JACQUELINE KENNEDY ONASSIS

Friend of the Arts

illustrated by Meryl Henderson

JACQUELINE KENNEDY ONASSIS

Friend of the Arts

by Beatrice Gormley

ALADDIN PAPERBACKS

New York London Toronto Sydney Singapore

First Aladdin Paperbacks edition September 2002
Text copyright © 2002 by Beatrice Gormley
Illustrations copyright © 2002 by Meryl Henderson

ALADDIN PAPERBACKS
An imprint of Simon & Schuster Children's Publishing Division
1230 Avenue of the Americas
New York, NY 10020

Designed by Lisa Vega
The text of this book was set in Adobe Garamond
Manufactured in the United States of America

4   6   8   10   9   7   5   3

Library of Congress Control Number: 2002107827

ISBN-13: 978-0-689-85295-4
ISBN-10: 0-689-85295-9
0713 OFF

ILLUSTRATIONS

CONTENTS

JACQUELINE KENNEDY ONASSIS

Friend of the Arts

An Aristocratic Family

It was a bright autumn day in 1933. The sky over Central Park in New York City was clear blue, and the trees glowed with orange and yellow leaves.

Along a path in the park skipped a girl about four years old. Her thick, curly dark hair was tied back on one side with a ribbon, and she wore a light coat over her dress. Behind the girl, a nanny pushed a baby carriage. Its wheels crunched over dry leaves.

"Don't get too far ahead of me, Jackie," warned the nanny.

"I won't, Miss Newey," said Jackie. She turned and skipped back. In the baby carriage her little sister, Lee, blinked at the world from under her pink bonnet. Jackie waved at Lee and skipped around the carriage. If she skipped *behind* Miss Newey, Jackie reasoned, she couldn't get ahead of her.

Miss Newey walked *so* slowly! Sometimes she even stopped to chat with other nannies. Jackie skipped backward, then forward again, then slowed to a walk. She noticed some fallen leaves on the grass, like orange and yellow stars.

And what was that gleaming under a different kind of leaf? A shiny brown horse chestnut. And another, and another . . . Jackie wandered across the grass, stooping to pick up the beautiful chestnuts and store them in her coat pockets.

As she came over a rise Jackie heard a baby crying. Down in a hollow, half-hidden by bushes, was a tarpaper shack. Jackie hesitated. Miss Newey had told her not to go near these shacks. "You are a very fortunate little girl," the nanny had added. "Think of the poor children who have to live like that."

As Jackie watched, a woman in a rumpled, dingy dress ducked out of the shack. She held a bundle of rags—no, it was a baby. That was where the crying came from.

The woman started to look up, and Jackie suddenly felt that she shouldn't be staring. Turning, she ran across the lawn. She should get back to Miss Newey and Baby Lee.

But now the path where the nanny and baby carriage had been was empty. Ahead, the path forked. One way climbed up a hill, and the other curved around behind evergreen shrubs.

Miss Newey must have gone over the hill, Jackie decided. Jackie would catch up with her quickly, so that the nanny wouldn't worry.

Briskly Jackie strode over the hill, under more trees, alongside a pond. The water shone brilliant blue. On a bench by the pond, a man in a shabby dark suit was stretched out, asleep. Miss Newey didn't want Jackie to go near those men who slept in the park either.

Then Jackie spotted a solid form in sensible coat and shoes—a nanny pushing a baby carriage. The back of the woman was disappearing through an arch. Jackie breathed a sigh of relief. "Miss Newey!"

she yelled to the figure and broke into a run.

But as the nanny glanced over her shoulder, Jackie saw that she wasn't Miss Newey. Jackie stopped short, swallowing hard. Where *was* Miss Newey?

The strange nanny looked back at her again. She must be wondering what a little girl was doing in the park all by herself. Putting her chin in the air, Jackie turned off on a side path. She would not show that she was worried.

When Mummy coached Jackie about riding her pony, she said the most important thing was to act as if you knew what you were doing. Then the horse would obey you. Now it seemed to Jackie that trying to find Miss Newey was like riding a horse. If Jackie acted as if she knew what she was doing . . .

There! Now Jackie did know what she was doing. Up ahead, near a lamppost, stood a man in a blue uniform—a policeman. Policemen were in the park to help people.

The policeman was already smiling at Jackie as she walked toward him. She spoke up clearly: "My nanny and my sister seem to be lost."

"Do they?" He stooped down to talk to her. "Well, don't worry—we'll find them. What's your name? Do you know your address—where you live?"

"My name is Jacqueline Bouvier," said Jackie. "I live in the apartment house where Ernest is the elevator man."

The policeman had Jackie repeat her name twice, Jahk-leen Boo-vee-ay. But he still didn't seem to understand. Didn't everyone in New York know the Bouviers?

"Tell you what—let's go along to the station," said the policeman, taking her hand. "That's where lost nannies usually end up."

As they walked out of the park, chatting, Jackie mentioned that she knew her telephone number. "Rhinelander 4-6167," she said. "You could call Mummy and tell her about Miss Newey and Baby Lee getting lost."

The policeman's lips twitched, but he said only, "Yes, I could. I think I will."

When they reached the police station, the officer sat Jackie up on a high stool. He picked up the

telephone and told the operator the Bouviers' number. Jackie listened to his side of the conversation. "Ma'am, we have a little girl here. I'm not sure of her name, but she gave us this telephone number. . . ."

Then the officer held the receiver to Jackie's ear. Mummy's voice, strangely high and strained, said, "Jacqueline? Darling, Mummy is taking a taxi to the police station. Wait right there!"

That was a silly thing to say—why would Jackie go somewhere else? She was having a fine time at the police station. The officers gathered around her stool, telling her what a brave, pretty little girl she was. "Where'd you get those dimples?" One of them gave her a piece of peppermint candy.

All too soon, a woman with hastily combed hair, wearing a fur-collared coat thrown around her shoulders, rushed into the station. "I am Mrs. John V. Bouvier III, and my daughter—" She stopped short, catching sight of Jackie on her stool.

"Hello, Mummy," said Jackie. She was surprised that her mother seemed upset, when Jackie had done exactly the right thing.

One day a year or so later, Jackie's grandfather John V. Bouvier Jr., took her to visit Great-uncle M. C. Bouvier and his wonderful art collection. It all happened because Jackie was reading when she was supposed to be taking a nap.

Before Lee was born, Jackie used to take naps in the nursery. Now Lee always napped in the nursery. Jackie was put in the guest room so the sisters wouldn't disturb each other.

Jackie knew there was no need for that. Even if Lee cried, she couldn't wake up Jackie—because Jackie didn't sleep at naptime. And Jackie wouldn't wake up Lee, because she knew how to be very, very quiet.

Now, after the spare room door was closed, Jackie waited a moment. Then she slipped off the bed and tiptoed over to the bookcase. The polished floor was smooth under her bare feet.

Jackie liked the books in the nursery, and she'd already memorized parts of *The Wonderful Wizard of Oz* and *Little Lord Fauntleroy*. But she thought the books in the spare room were even more interesting. One of Jackie's favorites was a book about ballet, with full-color pictures of ballerinas floating through the air. How did they do that? Mummy had promised to take her to the ballet this year.

Another book Jackie loved to look at was an art history book with reproductions of famous paintings. The words were hard to read, but the pictures—oh, she could stare at them for hours.

Jackie usually managed to jump back into bed as soon as she heard Miss Newey's footsteps in the hall. But this afternoon Jackie was enchanted by a painting of a girl on a swing. She didn't even hear the door open on its well-oiled hinges.

Miss Newey scolded Jackie for getting up from her nap, and for handling a valuable book without permission. Later she told Jackie's mother what Jackie had done. "Yes, Jacqueline," said Janet Bouvier, "you should have asked permission first." But she didn't seem angry—in fact, she looked proud.

The next time Jackie visited her Bouvier grandparents, Janet told them about Jackie reading the art book during naptime. Grandma Maude beamed at her. "It's Jacqueline's French artistic temperament coming out."

Grampy Jack, as Jackie called him, smiled too, under his gray mustache. He beckoned Jackie over to his chair. "So you like fine art, do you?"

Jackie smiled back at him. "Yes, Grampy Jack."

"If you liked the reproductions in a book, how would you like to see the real thing—real art treasures?"

"I would like it very much," said Jackie.

Not long after that, Grampy Jack took Jackie to visit Great-uncle M. C. Bouvier. They rode in a taxi to a brownstone house on West Forty-sixth Street. "Your great-uncle is not in good health," warned her grandfather as he lifted the brass knocker on the door.

A maid in black uniform and starched white apron showed them into the house. In the foyer, Jackie's Mary Janes stepped across thick red carpets. Huge gilt-framed mirrors hung on the walls, and Jackie's wide-eyed reflection stared back at her from both sides.

10

Jackie and her grandfather stepped through a doorway hung with heavy red velour curtains, tied back with gold-tasseled cords. In the drawing room M. C. Bouvier, a frail old man, greeted them from his armchair. Grampy Jack took Jackie around the room, pointing to each item with his manicured forefinger.

"These paintings are by the famous French artist Corot, and these by the famous French artist Millet. And this is a portrait of Louis Philippe, king of France. And the golden eagle over the fireplace was given to your great-great-great-grandfather Michel Bouvier by Joseph Bonaparte, brother of the Emperor Napoleon."

Jackie was dazzled, but not too dazzled to remember every last detail. That evening, when her father came home from the Stock Exchange, she told him all about it. "And there was an *horloge*— that's a clock, Daddy—of white marble and gilded bronze, with an eagle and sphinxes, and there was a beautiful glass chandelier made by Tiffany—why are you laughing, Daddy?"

Jack Bouvier put down his cigar, held out his

arms, and lifted Jackie onto his lap. "Only five years old, and what good taste you have! You love beautiful, costly things, don't you, my dear?"

Daddy seemed even more pleased with Jackie than Grampy Jack had been. "Oh, yes!" she answered.

"And you shall have them," he promised.

A Plucky Little Girl

The summer Jackie was five, she and her mother won third prize in the Family Class at the East Hampton Horse Show on Long Island. A picture of them on their matching chestnut mares was taken. The July day of that horse show was warm, but Janet and Jackie Bouvier were both correctly dressed in riding jackets, hats, and boots. Looking good, Jackie's mother explained, was as important as handling the horse well. You had to do both.

This summer, 1935, Jackie was six. She didn't need anyone else riding with her, and she was competing in the Southampton Horse Show on her own. "The other children in this jumping class will be quite a bit older," said Mummy to Jackie as they waited near the ring. "But that doesn't matter. All that matters is handling your pony correctly. Be sure to guide him straight at the fences, or he won't be able to make the jumps."

The first time around the ring, Jackie and her pony lifted perfectly over each fence. But the second time, Jackie glanced over at her mother sitting in the grandstand. Before she knew it, the pony was coming up on a fence crooked. In the next instant, the pony ducked the fence, Jackie lost her balance, and—*thump*—she was lying on the dirt.

Scrambling to her feet, Jackie grabbed the pony's reins. She had to get back in the saddle right away.

Then a man from the horse show was at her side, taking the reins from her. "Here, Jacqueline. You're mounting from the wrong side." His tone was kindly, but he was laughing.

Jackie's face burned with shame. How could she make such a stupid mistake on top of the first one? You *always* mounted from the left—she knew that. Grampy Jack had told her why: In medieval times, knights wore their swords on the left side of their belts.

Strangely, the crowd was clapping for her. They were smiling—everyone but her mother. Jackie heard a man exclaim, "What a plucky little girl!"

On the way home from the horse show, Jackie watched her mother drive. Mrs. Bouvier held the steering wheel of the dark blue Mercury convertible as surely as she held the reins of her favorite chestnut hunter, Danseuse. Whatever happened, Janet Lee Bouvier would never, ever, let *her* horse go at a fence crooked.

"Mummy," said Jackie suddenly, "why did they clap when I fell off?"

Janet pulled the car over to the side of the road and stopped. Even before she spoke, Jackie knew this was serious. "Those were terribly silly people," said her mother, looking at Jackie without smiling. "They didn't know what really happened. You should be ashamed of handling your pony so carelessly. He might have been hurt."

Jackie understood. Those people had clapped for her because they didn't expect much. They didn't know what a good rider a six-year-old could be. But Mummy knew, and she expected Jackie to do her best, always.

Every June, Janet Bouvier took Jackie and Lee and left New York City to spend the summer in East Hampton. They stayed at Wildmoor, a cottage owned by Grandfather Bouvier. It was near his beautiful estate, Lasata.

Grandfather James T. Lee and Grandmother Lee, Janet's parents, summered in East Hampton too. Sometimes Janet took Jackie and Lee to visit them. "Our nice apartment in New York really belongs to Grandfather Lee," Janet reminded her daughters. "It's very kind of him to let us live there."

But the Lee grandparents were strange, not like Grampy Jack and Grandmother Maude. The Bouvier grandparents had beautiful manners, and they behaved so courteously toward each other. Grandfather Lee had a short, sometimes rude way of speaking. And he didn't speak to Grandmother Lee at all. Also, Grandfather Lee smelled like the damp cigar he was always chewing. All in all, Jackie and Lee preferred to spend time at Lasata.

During the week Jack Bouvier had to work at the New York Stock Exchange, but he joined the family for the weekend. Jackie and Lee and their mother drove to the train station on Friday evenings to pick him up. One of those Fridays in the summer of 1936, Janet Bouvier and her daughters waited on the platform.

"Here comes the Cannonball!" Jackie shouted as soon as she heard the train's whistle. The Cannonball was Daddy's train. In a minute he'd be there, and the fun would begin. Jackie couldn't wait to tell him the latest about King Phar, their Great Dane.

Jack Bouvier stepped down from the train, deeply tanned and handsome as a movie star in his perfectly tailored white summer suit. The late-day sunlight gleamed on his slicked-down, middle-parted black hair.

"Daddy! Daddy!" Jackie ran up to her father with Lee close behind. "Guess what King Phar did at Mummy's bridge party? He wagged his tail and knocked all the drinks off the butler's table!"

Seizing the girls, their father swung them around.

"That King Phar—best dog in the world!" he laughed. He set his daughters down and bent to kiss his wife's cheek.

Janet Bouvier kept on smiling her public smile, but Jackie heard her say in a low voice, "You've been drinking."

At home, Jackie and Lee ate their supper in the kitchen. Their parents sat talking in the living room. Jackie listened to the voices in the other room, louder and louder and angrier and angrier. By the time the girls started their chocolate pudding, Jack and Janet Bouvier were shouting at each other. Jack said something sneering about "Old Man Lee." Janet shot back, "If it weren't for my father, we'd all be on the street."

Jackie looked across the kitchen table at Lee, only three years old. Her sister's big brown eyes reminded Jackie of a puppy's. Sliding out of her chair, Jackie took the little girl by the hand. "Come on, Lee. Let's go read *Winnie-the-Pooh*."

Upstairs in the nursery, Jackie sat cross-legged on the rug, and Lee knelt beside her. The curly dark head and the curly light brown head bent over the book. "'Chapter Five,'" read Jackie, "'In Which Piglet Meets a Heffalump.'"

Soon Jackie was deep into the story of how Pooh Bear and his friend Piglet tried to capture a Heffalump. Lee giggled helplessly as Jackie read Piglet's desperate cries: "'Help, help, a Herrible Hoffalump!"

Outside the story, downstairs in the living room, there was a splintering crash. Jackie could almost believe it was the sound of silly old Pooh Bear with his head stuck in the honey jar, smashing it against a root. Only a small part of her mind knew it was a whiskey glass shattering on the hearth. Louder than before, Jackie read on: "'Hoff, Hoff, a Hellible Horralump!'"

Later, when Jackie was in her nightgown and Lee was asleep in bed, Mummy and Daddy came to say good night. Janet kissed Jackie carefully, so as not to smudge her lipstick. There was a cloud of delicious perfume around her, and her silk dress rustled as she floated downstairs.

Jackie hugged her father goodnight. "Are you and Mummy going to a party at Lasata?"

"You bet, sweetheart." Jack Bouvier smelled like tobacco smoke and whiskey and the brilliantine oil on his black hair. "Someday you'll go to parties too." He chuckled. "You'll knock 'em dead."

When the front door closed behind her parents, Jackie ran to an upstairs window to watch them drive away. The engine of Jack Bouvier's Lincoln-Zephyr purred loudly, its tires crunched the gravel driveway, and they were off. Off to the party, a fairyland where elegant men and women swirled through soft lights and music. Someday Jackie too would wear a rustling dress and lovely perfume and swirl around the room, smiling at her partner.

A Thoroughbred

The November day was cool and overcast, but Jackie had pushed open a window in the apartment on Park Avenue. She and Lee were all dressed and ready for their Sunday with Daddy. Now they were waiting to hear his secret signal.

By the fall of 1936, Jack Bouvier didn't live with his wife and daughters any more. At the end of September, after one more terrible fight, Janet had made her husband move out. He now lived in a room in the Westbury Hotel, three blocks away on Madison Avenue.

Daddy didn't have any right to live in the expensive Park Avenue apartment, Mummy had told

Jackie and Lee, because it didn't belong to him. It belonged to Grandfather Lee. "Your father couldn't afford to buy a nice apartment like this," Mummy added.

Now Janet Bouvier walked into the room, frowning at the open window. "Where is that draft coming from?" she asked.

Just then, an automobile on the street below sounded a series of long and short toots. "That's Daddy!" exclaimed Jackie. "Come on, Lee. 'Bye, Mummy." The two girls ran out to the elevator, followed by their mother's last-minute instructions: "Keep your hats on! No sweets before dinner!"

A moment later Jackie and Lee were down at the curb, and their father was hugging them tight. "Now, let the good times roll, eh?" He ushered them into his car as if they were grand ladies.

As soon as they were around the corner from the apartment, Jackie pulled off her hat and tossed it into the back seat. "Did you ask the pet store about borrowing dogs, Daddy?"

"You bet, sweetie. It's all arranged." He parked the car in front of a pet store near Central Park.

24

"The man says we can borrow three dogs, one for each of us. You can choose any dog in the store."

The girls rushed into the pet store, greeted by excited barking. "I choose this one," said Jackie, stroking the head of a white bull terrier puppy.

Taking out his wallet, Jack Bouvier gave the store owner a deposit, in case the dogs got lost. Jackie and Lee clipped leashes on the three dogs. Then the six of them scampered happily out of the store and into the park.

Jackie and Lee and their father spent the morning racing up and down the paths, with the joyful dogs in the lead. As they returned the dogs to the pet store, Jackie felt a pang for her father. She knew he missed their dogs. He couldn't keep a dog in his room at the Westbury Hotel. She squeezed his hand.

"Are we going to Schraft's for lunch, Daddy?" asked Lee.

"Absolutely." Jack Bouvier beamed at his second daughter. "And then we'll go to a movie."

The movie was *The Call of the Wild*. Clark Gable played a fearless, handsome man who was friends with a brave dog. Lee was really too young to sit

through a feature movie, and she squirmed and finally dozed off. But Jackie was entranced every minute. When they came out of the theater into the pale late-afternoon sunlight, she was in a daze.

Glancing up at her dark, handsome father, Jackie exclaimed, "Daddy—you look just like Clark Gable!"

Jack Bouvier's teeth gleamed under his little mustache, and he squeezed her shoulders. "Really? I thought he looked just like *me*." He steered Jackie and Lee toward the door of a drugstore. "Here's a soda fountain. How about a hot fudge sundae before I have to give up the best daughters a man ever had?"

As Daddy was about to drop them off at Park Avenue, Jackie fished their hats from the back seat. She pushed them down over her and Lee's wild hair. Taking her handkerchief, Jackie wiped the chocolate from the corners of Lee's mouth. Unfortunately Lee had dripped chocolate sauce on her new white blouse too, but maybe Mummy wouldn't notice.

Upstairs in the apartment, Janet Bouvier greeted them. "Well, did you have a nice Sunday? What did you do with Daddy?"

Although their mother was smiling as she unbuttoned Lee's coat, Jackie felt cautious. But Lee babbled on about the dogs and the park and the movie and how Daddy looked exactly like the movie star, and just as Lee was going to blurt out about the sundaes in the drugstore, Jackie gave her a nudge.

But it didn't matter. With Lee's coat half-unbuttoned, Mummy paused. She stared at the chocolate smears on the front of Lee's blouse. "I see your father fed you ice cream just before dinner," she said in an icy tone.

The girls had to stand there while Janet Bouvier paced the foyer of the apartment, getting angrier and angrier. "It's fine for *him* to stuff you with sweets and spoil your appetites. It's fine for *him* to let you run through the park without your hats—I can tell perfectly well, Jacqueline, that your hair did not get in that wild state from wearing a hat. Then, when you get sick, who has to nurse you?"

"Miss Kemmerle does," said Jackie, as if she were giving an answer in class.

At that, Janet looked so angry that Jackie thought

she was going to slap her. "Don't you dare speak back to me." She started to raise her hand. Then she dropped it, whirled, and stalked off.

Lee began to sob out loud. "I wish we could be with Daddy all the time!"

Ever since she had turned six, Jackie had gone to Miss Chapin's School, a private girls' school on the Upper East Side of Manhattan. This morning, as usual, the halls of Chapin hummed with chatter. Girls in blue linen jumpers, the school uniform, clattered up and down the stairs on their way to class.

Jackie, eight years old now, wore a jumper like everyone else, but she didn't like it. She wasn't the same as all the other girls—why should she have to dress like them? Unlike the others, Jackie was headed for the headmistress's office. Her homeroom teacher had met her at the classroom door and taken her aside. "Jacqueline, Miss Stringfellow would like to see you in her office."

Even though the teacher had spoken quietly, at least two other girls had heard. By the time Jackie returned from the headmistress's office, the whole class would know.

This didn't bother Jackie one bit, though. She already had a reputation as the naughtiest girl in the school. She would race through her classwork and then find some kind of mischief to get into.

If a teacher left the classroom for a moment, Jackie might jump up and give a funny imitation of her. Sometimes, when no one was looking, funny drawings would appear on the blackboard. Jackie argued with the other students, naturally: If Jackie was right and they were wrong, why should she be polite about it?

Jackie's mother had even had a conference with Miss Stringfellow about her daughter's behavior. But in Jackie's opinion, it was nothing to worry about. Just her French temperament coming out, as Grandmother Maude liked to say.

Sitting on a straight chair in front of Miss Stringfellow's oak desk, Jackie folded her hands in the lap of her jumper. As she expected, the headmistress began, "Jacqueline, I've heard bad reports about you."

With a serious expression, Jackie focused her large, wide-set eyes on Miss Stringfellow's face. She knew from past experience that the headmistress would lecture her for a while. Jackie wouldn't listen, but every once in a while she would nod and say, "Yes, Miss Stringfellow." Finally the headmistress would send her back to homeroom. And that would be that—until the next time Jackie misbehaved.

But this time Miss Stringfellow had a thoughtful look on her face. She leaned forward, her hands flat on her desk blotter. "You love horses, don't you, Jacqueline? You love to ride, and I understand you've already won some prizes in the ring."

"Yes, Miss Stringfellow." This was something different. What did horses have to do with Jackie's pranks?

"Then maybe you'll understand when I say that you yourself are like a beautiful thoroughbred. You can run fast. You have staying power. You're well built and you have brains."

Jackie sat up a little straighter. She hadn't thought of herself as a thoroughbred horse, but she had to agree it was true.

"But if you're not properly trained," Miss Stringfellow went on in a more serious tone, "you'll be good for nothing."

Nothing? Jackie was shocked. Now she was listening to every word.

"Suppose you owned the most beautiful race horse in the world," said the headmistress. "What good would he be if he wasn't trained to stay on the track, to stand still at the starting gate, to obey commands? He couldn't even pull a milk truck or a trash cart. He would be useless to you, and you would have to get rid of him."

"Yes, Miss Stringfellow," said Jackie. The headmistress was telling her in so many words, *If you won't behave, you will have to leave Chapin School.* Jackie didn't want that to happen.

Jackie walked slowly back to her homeroom, thinking about what Miss Stringfellow had said. There was something very important at stake here, even more important than whether she would be expelled from Chapin School. Miss Stringfellow was telling Jackie what a shameful waste it would be if she didn't discipline herself. Jackie had to admit, she would never allow a horse of hers to misbehave and waste its talents. But she had been spoiling herself just that way.

After that meeting, Jackie's pranks stopped. She earned straight As in every class. Jackie was determined to show the headmistress what a thoroughbred girl could do when she put her mind to it.

In the summer of 1937 Jack Bouvier talked his wife into living with him again. He rented a cottage for the four of them in East Hampton, close to Grandfather Bouvier's estate, Lasata.

Jack and Janet Bouvier didn't get along any better than before. But the girls stayed away from their parents as much as they could. Lee spent most of her time bicycling with friends or frolicking with her Bouvier cousins in the surf at the Maidstone Club.

As for Jackie, every day she put on her riding outfit, braided her unruly curls, and went to the Lasata stables. She spent hours practicing in the ring, because the Southampton Horse Show was coming up in July. She was determined to be the best in her division, children under nine.

Besides, Jackie would rather be with the horses than with anyone else. She loved everything about them: the way they whickered to greet her, their warm horsey scent, the way their coats shone when she groomed them. And it was thrilling, the way they followed her slightest movements when she rode.

The day of the Southampton Horse Show, Jackie won her class. In the grandstand, Mummy and Daddy beamed down at her instead of fighting with each other. Grampy Jack and Grandma Maude were glowing with pride too. All the cousins, even the older ones, sat on the fences cheering for her.

Most important of all, Jackie knew she had done her best. Taking her blue ribbon from the judge, Jackie knew this was the way she wanted to feel about herself—always. Miss Stringfellow had understood.

By the Booming Blue Sea

By the fall of 1937 Jack and Janet Bouvier had completely given up on their marriage. From then on, they lived apart. At the beginning of the summer of 1938, Janet Bouvier took Jackie and Lee to Long Island as usual. But instead of going to East Hampton with the Bouvier clan, she rented a cottage in Bellport, several miles away.

"Of course Bellport isn't fashionable," Janet told the girls, "but it's all I can afford with my stingy payments from your father." Jackie hated it when her mother talked that way. It made Jackie's stomach knot up, hearing about what they could afford and what they couldn't.

Jackie and Lee didn't miss the awful fights their parents had last summer, but they longed to be with their father and grandparents and cousins. Sometimes they read books, and sometimes they drew or painted. Janet encouraged them to do artistic things, although she herself couldn't draw.

Sometimes the girls played pretend games, using stories from their books. "I'll be Mary, Queen of Scots," Jackie would say to Lee on one of the long afternoons when their mother was out playing bridge. Mary, Queen of Scots, was a brave queen who had been beheaded by the cruel English. "You can be my lady-in-waiting."

Often when Janet Bouvier came home from a bridge luncheon, she changed her clothes and went out again until late at night. But sometimes she would be home for dinner, and then the girls had to speak French at the table. It was like a game—each girl had ten matches at her place for counters. If you spoke an English word by mistake, you had to give up a match. Jackie liked this game, and she didn't lose many matches.

At the end of July, Janet had to let Jack take the

girls to East Hampton for the rest of the summer. One glorious morning, Jack Bouvier pulled up in front of Janet's cottage with the top of his convertible down. "On to Lasata!" shouted Jackie as the car roared down the road. "On to Lasata!" echoed Lee, squeezed between Jackie and their father in the front seat. The wind whipped the girls' hair.

August 12 was Grampy Jack's birthday—he was turning seventy-three. Jackie had written a poem for him, bordered with drawings.

They all dressed up for the birthday lunch, of course. The boy cousins wore blue blazers, white linen trousers, shirts, and ties. Jackie, Lee, and all the other girl cousins wore their best dresses with long sleeves, white knee socks, and patent-leather shoes. Grandmother Maude was always beautifully dressed in her sweet, soft, old-fashioned way. Grampy Jack himself appeared in a tailored suit with a high starched shirt collar and a jeweled stickpin in his tie. His mustache was neatly waxed.

Before lunch, Jack Bouvier mixed cocktails for the adults. Then they all went into the dining room, where family portraits hung on the walls. The long oak table, big enough for the whole Bouvier clan, was spread with the finest lace table-cloth. At a nod from Grampy Jack at the head of the table, the boys and men pulled out chairs for the girls and women. Even the youngest girls allowed themselves to be seated like little ladies, smoothing their skirts underneath.

The appetizer was tomatoes (sweet, ripe Lasata-grown tomatoes) stuffed with crabmeat. The main course was roast Long Island duckling, baby Lima beans, and corn on the cob. Those vegetables, too, were from Lasata's own gardens.

After the main course was served, Jack Bouvier called down the long table to his father. "What do you think of our Jackie? Straight As in school and blue ribbons in the horse shows. And she's the prettiest thing in the ring, to boot."

Grampy Jack had just taken a forkful of duck-ling, so he merely nodded and smiled. Jackie beamed at her father. If Mummy were here, she would try to stop Daddy from bragging. But Jackie loved to hear him say how wonderful she was.

"She *might* be the prettiest," Jackie heard a cousin whisper, "if she weren't bowlegged."

There were giggles from the children, and their parents didn't scold them. Grampy Jack wouldn't stand for rude remarks at his table, but he couldn't hear them, even with his hearing aid turned on.

"And if she didn't have such gigantic feet," said another cousin. More giggles.

Jackie had to pretend she didn't care, but Daddy actually seemed to like getting a rise out of the cousins. "Jealous," he said, and he smiled.

After the servants had cleared the plates, the birthday cake made its entrance with homemade peach ice cream and homemade chocolate sauce. Aunt Edie, Jack Bouvier's older sister, led everyone in singing "Happy Birthday to You." Aunt Edie was peculiar, and Jackie knew that Mummy didn't like her and Lee to visit her at Grey Gardens, her house in East Hampton. But Aunt Edie certainly could sing. People said she might have been a famous soprano, if Grampy Jack had let her have a career.

As soon as the children were excused from the table, the cousins wandered outside to play with the dogs. But Jackie ran upstairs to change into her riding clothes and raced out to the stables. "Here I am," she called to her pony. The pony whickered an answer from her stall.

That August of 1938 was warm and sunny, and it seemed that the flowerbeds in the Italian garden at Lasata had never bloomed so luxuriously. Day after day Jackie swam at the beach in the morning and rode in the afternoon. Jack Bouvier took the whole month off from his Wall Street job so that he could be with his daughters.

But the next summer, when Jackie turned ten, the weather in East Hampton was often cool and overcast. It seemed as if the cloud of unhappiness from their battling parents had followed Jackie and Lee even to Lasata. Her mother's and father's voices, yelling, echoed in Jackie's head. *More money! Scandal! Divorce!*

Jackie knew that her cousins discussed her parents' marriage, and most of the time she kept a distance from them. She spent many rainy days that August curled up with a book, writing poems, or sketching pictures.

Again the family celebrated Grampy Jack's birthday, but this time it was a dark, damp day. However, Grampy Jack had a special present for each grandchild. He had updated and republished his book, *Our Forebears*, about the Bouvier family history.

When Jackie came up to her grandfather to receive her copy, he gave her a special smile. "We are of noble stock, Jacqueline," he said. "Never forget that."

Her face glowing, Jackie opened her copy to read her grandfather's inscription to her, a little verse.

Grampy Jack picked up an old volume lying beside the stack of *Our Forebears*. "Pay attention, children," he told his assembled grandchildren. "Here is the Bouvier coat of arms, from *The Armorial de Dauphiné*." Adjusting his pince-nez glasses on his nose, he found the place and turned the book so the children could see. On a blue shield a medieval-looking lion stretched out its claws. *"D'azur au lion d'or,"* he read, savoring the French words on his tongue.

"D'azur au lion d'or," whispered Jackie. She

loved French. She was determined to learn to speak it as if she'd grown up in the land of her ancestors.

Later, alone in her room, Jackie pored over *Our Forebears*. It seemed that Grampy Jack's grandmother Louise Vernou came from stock even more noble than the Bouviers. "Illustrious and ancient," he called the Vernous. One of them had been knighted by Louis XIV, the brilliant Sun King of France!

On the overcast days when it wasn't actually raining, Jackie sometimes went to the beach by herself. She stood at the edge of the damp sand, her eyes almost closed against the wind, and listened to the waves crashing over and over. It felt as if the surf was surging through her, washing out her parents' screaming voices and her cousins' whispers.

The winter of 1939–40 was drearier than Lasata could ever be, even on the rainiest, darkest days. Janet and Jackie and Lee were no longer living on Park Avenue. Grandfather Lee, who owned that apartment, had made them move to a smaller apartment on Gracie Square. Grandfather Lee often visited Janet there, and they had long talks about "What to Do." Lee didn't seem to understand—except that she missed Daddy, of course.

But Jackie knew well enough what her mother and Grandfather Lee were planning. One evening her father came to the apartment and Jackie overheard the adults talking. Shouting, rather. It made Jackie think of a dogfight. Daddy was a handsome pedigreed dog like their Great Dane, King Phar. Grandfather Lee and Mummy were like mongrels snarling and backing Daddy into a corner. "Grounds for divorce," growled Grandfather Lee.

Jackie couldn't stand to listen any more. The words hurt her, more than falling off a horse would hurt. Rushing up the stairs, Jackie bumped into Bernice Anderson, the maid, in the hall.

"Why, Jackie," said Bernice. "What is it?"

"I hate my mother." Pushing past Bernice, Jackie shut the door of her room. She sat down on the bed and stared at the wall for several minutes. Then Jackie opened a drawer and took out a poem she had written . It was titled "Sea Joy." The poem expressed how much she wanted to live "by the booming blue sea."

Jackie had decorated the side margins of the page with starfish and seaweed. At the top of the page she drew a sketch of herself at the edge of the waves. Her face was tilted up to the wind, her hair blowing back. Gulls wheeled overhead. Jackie wished more than anything that she could be there, right now.

Next weekend Jackie gave the illustrated poem to her father. "Talented as well as beautiful, eh?" he said. He put an arm around her shoulders and gave her a squeeze. "We have some good times at the beach, don't we, sweetheart?"

A Crack in the Social Register

One morning toward the end of January 1940, Jackie went to school as usual. Janet Bouvier was sleeping in, and Jackie's governess walked her the short distance from the Gracie Square apartment to the school. The morning was bleak and icy, and her ran up the front steps to get out of the cold.

Inside, something made Jackie pause to look at a cluster of girls in the hall. They were in the class above her. One girl was reading out loud to the others from a newspaper clipping. "'A line in the Social Register will be cracked right in two if Mrs. Janet Lee Bouvier of One Gracie Square has her way.'"

Another girl caught sight of Jackie and nudged

the reader, who stopped. Raising her chin, Jackie brushed by those hateful girls as if they weren't there. Still, amid the giggles she caught the words "adultery" and "Black Jack."

The Bouviers' private life was spread all over the papers. How could Mummy do this to Jackie and Lee? How could she do it to Daddy?

Jackie didn't care what those stupid girls were saying. She wasn't even listening—she was on her way to homeroom.

But as Jackie stepped into her homeroom, there were more snickers, more sideways glances. Hanging up her coat and scarf, Jackie slid into her seat beside her best friend, Nancy Tuckerman. "Hi, Tuckie." She gave her friend a defiant stare. If Nancy said *one word* about what those girls were enjoying so much, the friendship would be over.

"Hi, Jackie." Tuckie must have known about the shameful news. But she said only, "Did you ask your father about riding this weekend?"

Something inside Jackie relaxed a little. She had one friend, at least. "Daddy said sure, if it doesn't snow."

That afternoon, on her way back home, Jackie saw the newspaper headline for herself. A newsboy was holding up a paper and shouting, "Read all about it! Society broker sued for divorce!"

Jackie shrank further inside herself. She drew herself far away from this shame and misery, like a princess high in a tower in a faraway land.

At the end of the school year in June, Janet took Jackie and Lee to a dude ranch near Reno, Nevada. The girls had never been out West, and it was an adventure for them. Jackie loved galloping across the desert on a mustang pony. For her mother, though, the trip was serious work. Janet was determined to end her marriage to Jack Bouvier, but in those days it was very difficult to get a divorce in New York or most other states. Nevada was the only state in the country where you could get a divorce in a matter of weeks, just by living there. In July, the divorce was final, and Janet was free to remarry.

Janet, Jackie, and Lee returned east, to East Hampton. The girls would spend August with their father and the rest of the Bouviers, while their mother stayed with Grandfather Lee. Jackie was glad to be at Lasata, but she felt uncomfortable around her cousins. Like the girls at Chapin, they gossiped and giggled about Jack and Janet's divorce.

Jackie even overheard Aunt Michelle laughing with Jackie's father. "I hear she's going out with some man or other every night," said Jack. He swished his glass, making the ice cubes clink.

"Yes, the Great Manhunt is on!" said Michelle. She made a bugling sound, like a hunting horn. Jackie cringed with shame. "The Great Manhunt," she knew, meant Janet Bouvier's search for a new husband.

More than ever, Jackie sought refuge in the stables. She was big enough and a good enough rider now to handle her mother's chestnut mare, Danseuse. Jackie would come into the stable with an apple in her pocket, and Danseuse—Donny, Jackie called her—would snuffle softly. She knew Jackie had a treat for her.

Sometimes Jackie would just stand with her arms around Donny, pressing her head against the animal's neck. The warmth and strength of the horse

seemed to flow into Jackie's body. Sometimes she stroked Donny's white blaze and kissed the soft pink spot at the end of her nose. "You know how lovely you are, don't you?" Jackie whispered.

In the riding ring, mounted on her chestnut hunter, Jackie felt powerful. Everything else in the world faded away as Jackie and Danseuse soared over one fence after the other. They were perfectly free, in perfect control.

In years past Janet had won many blue ribbons and trophy cups mounted on Danseuse. This summer it was Jackie and Danseuse who won two major prizes at the horse shows on Long Island, the Alfred B. Maclay Trophy for horsemanship and the Good Hands competition. That meant Jackie qualified for the finals at the big Madison Square Garden Show in New York City in the fall.

And that October everyone in society knew that Jacqueline Bouvier was a champion rider. She swept the field of twenty other young finalists, boys and girls. The day after the show, Mummy's face broke into a smile as she opened the *New York Times*. She read aloud: "'Miss Bouvier'—that's you, darling—

'achieved a rare distinction. The occasions are few when a young rider wins both contests in the same show.'"

The following spring, 1941, Janet Bouvier took Jackie and Lee on a trip to Washington, D.C. "Aren't the cherry blossoms lovely?" said their mother. "The trees were planted by President Taft's wife, you know. Isn't it generous of Grandfather Lee to give us this trip?"

The cherry trees were lovely, and Jackie was thrilled by the paintings and sculpture in the National Gallery of Art. But touring the White House was a letdown. The president's mansion reminded Jackie of a big hotel—and not a very well-kept hotel, at that. "Well, what can you expect from a First Lady like Mrs. Roosevelt?" remarked Janet. She ran a white-gloved finger along the top of a sideboard, and shook her head at the smear of gray dust. "Mrs. Roosevelt spends all her time traveling around the country and writing her newspaper columns. Now, if *I* were the lady of this house, I'd have a few words with the servants."

The dust was unfortunate, but what bothered Jackie much more was how drab and ordinary the furnishings were. The White House ought to be filled with beautiful things, she thought, like the National Gallery was. And visiting the White House ought to make Americans proud of their history, the way visiting Lasata made Jackie proud of her family history. Being here in Washington made Jackie want to learn more about all the American presidents and their wives and families. But there was nothing in the White House to teach her—not even a booklet to take home and read.

During their week in Washington, Janet went out almost every evening. Jackie knew these dates must be part of what her aunts called the Great Manhunt. Last year her mother had gone out for a time with a man named Mr. Zinsser, and at Lasata they joked that Janet had gone "from A to Z" in her search for a rich husband.

Now, although Jackie and Lee didn't know it yet, Janet was back to "A." She was dating Hugh D. Auchincloss, a wealthy stockbroker.

A New Family

On December 7, 1941, Japan attacked Pearl Harbor. Suddenly the United States was at war with Japan and Nazi Germany.

In Jackie's personal life, too, the last month of 1941 marked a big change. Instead of spending Christmas in New York, as they always had, Janet and Jackie and Lee went to Washington, D.C. "I want you to meet a very good friend of mine, Mr. Hugh D. Auchincloss," Janet told the girls as they packed for the trip. "He's very sweet, and everyone calls him Hughdie. He's invited us to stay at his lovely estate, Merrywood, for a few days, and he'll show us around Washington, D.C. I think it would be nice if you called him 'Uncle Hughdie.'"

Glancing at her sister's glum face, Jackie knew Lee didn't think it would be nice. Neither did Jackie. They both wished they could stay in New York and have a holiday lunch with Daddy. Poor Daddy, all by himself in his apartment!

But when Jackie and Lee met Hugh D. Auchincloss and one of his sons, Yusha, they had to admit they liked them both. Mr. Auchincloss was a large, calm, kindly man. A bit boring, Jackie thought. Maybe that was what her mother wanted, though, after years of unpleasant excitement with Jack Bouvier.

Yusha, two years older than Jackie, was shy but very nice. Yusha was someone Jackie could talk to about serious things. Like Jackie, he read and thought a great deal about the war raging in Europe. He wanted to drop out of his preparatory school, Groton, and join the Marines.

Yusha took the girls to see Arlington National Cemetery, across the river from Washington, D.C. At the Tomb of the Unknown Soldier, Jackie was impressed with the ceremonial guard. Standing on a hill in the cemetery, she and Yusha talked again about the war. "Men *we* know might die in battle and be buried here," said Yusha.

Jackie was silent for a moment, looking out over the city. "But if they have to die, what a peaceful place to be."

The Auchincloss estate, Merrywood, was also on the Virginia shore of the Potomac River. During the visit Jackie and Yusha took long walks through the woods and fields, discussing the war. Jackie was especially caught up with the French Resistance to the German Nazis. "I think General Charles de Gaulle is the noblest man in the world," said Jackie. They were standing on a bluff overlooking the river, and to Jackie the inspiring scenery seemed to be connected with her inspiring French hero.

In June 1942 Janet Lee Bouvier became Mrs. Hugh D. Auchincloss. Jackie and Lee joined the Auchincloss family at Hammersmith Farm, their summer home in Newport, Rhode Island. Hammersmith Farm was several times as large as Grandfather Bouvier's estate, Lasata, and even more luxurious. And in the fall, Jackie and Lee

moved to their mother's new home, Merrywood. The girls had to drop out of Chapin in New York and begin at new private day schools. Jackie went to Holton-Arms in Washington, D.C, and Lee to McLean School in Virginia. They could visit their father in New York, but Merrywood was where they lived now.

One misty Saturday morning that autumn, Jackie was in her yellow-and-white third-floor bedroom pulling on her riding clothes. Lee, still in her nightgown, leaned against the doorway of her sister's room and said, "I wish we were still in New York."

Jackie raised her eyebrows, signaling, *Go ahead, tell me what's bothering you.*

"Nini hates me." Nini was their eight-year-old stepsister, Nina.

"Oh, Nini! She's just a baby," said Jackie. "She stuck her tongue out at *me* last night, but who cares?"

Lee twirled a strand of her curly hair around her finger, meaning that she had more to say. "I miss Chapin."

"I know," said Jackie, starting to braid her own

hair. "But Holton-Arms isn't bad—you'll like it when you get there. Miss Shearman—she's the Latin teacher—is a slave driver, though!"

"I miss New York," said Lee in a small voice.

"I know," said Jackie again. "But don't you just love Merrywood? We have everything here—stables so I can ride whenever I want to, and a swimming pool—*you're* the one who loves to swim so much—and acres and acres of woods and fields to ride through. And the view of the river from the bluff!" Lee's eyes were filling with tears, so Jackie rushed on. "And can you believe Mummy let us choose the colors of our rooms? Your blue room is so pretty."

Lee nodded, but then she sniffled. "I miss seeing Daddy on weekends."

"I miss Daddy too," said Jackie. "And he misses us." She'd gotten one of his sad letters just the other day. He said his only satisfaction in life now was talking to Jackie and Lee on the phone or getting letters from them. As she read the letter, Jackie could picture him sitting at his early nineteenth-century French desk. He'd write a few lines, then set down his pen to pick up his glass of whiskey.

No—Jackie didn't want to picture that. Quickly she went on to her sister, "Oh, Lee—know what I learned in Spanish? A swear word: *caramba!*" Jackie repeated it, stamping her riding boot and sticking her chest out like a bullfighter. "And you have to really roll the R: *carrramba!*"

"*Carrramba!*" exclaimed Lee, imitating Jackie. The girls stamped around the chintz-curtained room, snapping their fingers and swearing in Spanish.

Later in the fall Jackie and Lee finally had a chance to spend a weekend in New York with their father. Jack Bouvier sulked as though he were no older than Nini. "I suppose your mother thinks she's hit the jackpot, marrying Mr. Stuffed Shirt," he sneered as they strolled along Fifth Avenue. "Mr. Big-time Stockbroker. You know what I tell the boys at the Stock Exchange? I tell them, 'Take a loss with Auchincloss.'"

Jackie smiled, but she said nothing. Her father, she knew, was the one who'd taken losses on the Stock Exchange. Otherwise, why would he live in a little two-bedroom apartment? Uncle Hughdie owned an apartment on Park Avenue in New York *and* his Virginia estate, Merrywood. *And* his family owned Hammersmith Farm in fashionable Newport, Rhode Island.

"What about you girls—do you like living with the snobs down there? I'll tell you what they don't have in Washington: They don't have Sak's Fifth Avenue." Jack Bouvier paused outside the fashionable department store. In the window, the mannequins posed to show off their winter dresses and coats.

"Oh, Daddy—could we go in the store and look?" Jackie loved the clothes in Sak's. So did her father, she knew.

"Why not?" said Jack Bouvier. "No harm in looking."

Walking into the store, Jackie breathed in the thrilling smell of new fabric. The sales clerks welcomed her and Lee and their father like special guests. Speaking to Jack Bouvier in low, pleasant tones, the clerks ushered the girls into the dressing room to try on clothes .

Some time later Jack Bouvier and his daughters walked out of Sak's. Jackie and Lee each carried a beautiful new dress, nestled in tissue paper in one of Sak's special boxes. With that box under her arm, Jackie felt that *she* was special too.

During the next two years Jackie settled into her new life with the Auchinclosses. She enjoyed everything about Merrywood—the sound of the river flowing endlessly by, the steep hills, even the path to the stable with the stones that slipped as she ran up it. She loved Hammersmith Farm, with its spacious green fields and the summer wind sighing through the grass. She loved the sound of the foghorns at night as she went to sleep in her yellow-and-white bedroom. Both those estates had a peaceful, settled feeling, as if they would be there, unchanging, forever.

Each August Jackie spent with her father in East Hampton, where she'd spent so many summers. But East Hampton no longer seemed like the place where she belonged. Lasata was the same, but Jackie herself felt more like a visitor.

At the Maidstone Club one morning in August 1944, Jackie came out of the dressing room in her swimsuit. Some boys were hanging around the cabana, trying to look casual. Jackie saw immediately that they were waiting for *her*.

She also noticed her father on the terrace in his lounge chair, a drink on the table beside him. His already dark skin glistened with suntan oil. From behind his sunglasses he watched Jackie and the boys with a grin.

"Hey, Jackie, where're you going to school this year?" asked one of the boys. "Down in Washington?"

"No, I'm going away to Miss Porter's, in Connecticut." Jackie smiled sweetly at the boys, but she didn't stop to talk. She saw the boys' admiring glances, but she didn't admire them back or want to spend time with them. Jackie had turned fifteen. She was going away to boarding school.

She'd rather talk to older men like Prince Serge Obolensky, a friend of the Bouviers. He told fascinating stories about his life in Russia before the revolution. Why would she want to hang around with these clumsy, boring boys, when she could talk to a prince?

Jacqueline Could Do Better

Miss Porter's, a private boarding school for girls in Farmington, a charming New England town, was fashionable and expensive. It was also an excellent college preparatory school. A great deal was expected of a student at Miss Porter's, Jackie soon found out. Even when she did well in her classes, the headmaster wrote on her reports, "Jacqueline could do better."

On her letters home to her mother, Jackie drew mocking pictures of the headmaster in the margins. She entertained the other girls by imitating his voice: "Jacqueline could do better." At the same time, Jackie did want to do better. She especially loved her courses in art history, English, and literature, because those teachers expected so much of her.

During her first year in Farmington, Grampy Jack wrote Jackie a letter about what *he* expected of her. He talked about her preparation at Miss Porter's for "future feats of work and responsibility." Jackie, he felt, was someone who could become a leader, and this was a serious responsibility. "Before leading others, we must guide and direct ourselves. This is the true way of usefulness in life."

Jackie was glad to see old friends at Miss Porter's: her cousin Shella, and Nancy Tuckerman from Chapin School. She badly missed her favorite horse, though. Her mother wouldn't pay for Danseuse to be stabled in Connecticut. The Auchinclosses could easily afford the stabling fees, of course, but Janet didn't believe in spoiling her children by giving them everything they wanted. So Jackie wrote a pleading letter to Grampy Jack—and soon Donny joined Jackie at Miss Porter's.

Miss Porter's School didn't require uniforms like the Chapin School, but most of the girls wore the same clothes anyway. For instance, there seemed to be an unwritten rule that everyone had to wear a white rain slicker. Jackie ignored that rule and all the other unwritten rules about clothes. She didn't play team sports either, or spend her free time socializing with the other girls. When the other girls gathered in the evenings, Jackie read or painted in her room. While they were playing field hockey, Jackie was exercising Danseuse.

During Jackie's second year, she and Tuckie roomed together. One Saturday morning, the two girls spruced up for a special outing. Jack Bouvier was driving up from New York to take Jackie, Tuckie, and his niece Shella to lunch. Jackie stood in front of her mirror, brushing her springy dark hair.

"I can't wait," moaned Tuckie, flopping onto her bed. "The Elm Tree Inn! Your father is *divine*. He treats like Daddy Warbucks, and he looks like Clark Gable."

Setting down her brush, Jackie gazed at the picture of her father on the dresser. It had been taken on vacation in Havana, Cuba, in the 1920s. Deeply tanned, wearing a sporty tropical suit, Jack Bouvier lurked among the palm trees like a panther.

"I know," said Jackie. Daddy was paying for Danseuse to be boarded in Farmington now. He would do anything to make her happy.

Jackie *was* happy that afternoon, sitting in the dining room of the Elm Tree Inn. She was proud of her father, dressed in one of his beautifully tailored double-breasted suits, smiling around the table at the girls. With their best Miss Porter's table manners, they had each devoured a Porterhouse steak and a hot fudge sundae. "Those Elm Tree Inn desserts are skimpy, aren't they, ladies?" asked Jack Bouvier. "More sundaes all around?"

Early in 1945 Janet and Hughdie's first child, Janet Jennings Auchincloss, was born. Traveling to Washington for the baptism, Jackie presented her mother with one of her illustrated poems. "The Baby of the Year," she called little Janet.

The poem went on and on, in the rhythm of "The Midnight Ride of Paul Revere," getting more unlikely as it went. One line predicted that Baby Janet would become the first woman President. The family laughed heartily at that, looking at this baby in her long white christening dress.

Jackie had written the poem to please her mother and Uncle Hughdie. But now that she saw her baby half sister, she was truly delighted with her. Propping Baby Janet on her knees, Jackie coaxed a smile from her. Little children were sort of like dogs, she thought. It made you feel light-hearted just to be with them.

That April, as the United States and its allies were on the verge of winning World War II, President Franklin Delano Roosevelt died. From the time Jackie was a little girl, she'd heard bad things about President Roosevelt. Grampy Jack had always grumbled about FDR "taxing our family out of existence." Jack Bouvier heartily hated Roosevelt, most of all for his Securities and Exchange Commission, headed by "that crook" Joe Kennedy in the 1930s. "The Democrats don't want an honest stockbroker to make a decent living," Jackie's father had complained.

But Jackie had her own opinions, and she was

stunned at the death of this powerful leader. "I think he was really great," she wrote to her stepbrother Yusha, at Groton. What would happen to the country, she wondered, now that Roosevelt was dead? Who could replace him?

Also, poor Mrs. Roosevelt! Besides losing her husband, she had to leave the White House, where she had lived for twelve years. It must be awfully hard.

In her three years at Miss Porter's, Jackie did take part in some activities other than reading and riding. She acted in school plays—she felt more at home on a stage in front of an audience than she did in a room with girls her age. She worked on the school newspaper, the *Salamagundy*, writing stories and poems and drawing cartoons. Jackie made up a cartoon character, Frenzied Frieda, who got into one scrape after another.

Jackie felt lucky that the Lewises, Uncle Hughdie's cousin and her husband, a well-known scholar, happened to live in Farmington. They often invited Jackie and her friends over for tea. It was good just to get away from school for a little while, Jackie thought, but the best thing about going to the Lewises was their private library. The Lewises were pleased that Jackie was so interested in their collection, and they gave her some beautiful art books for Christmas presents.

Reading about art and history, Jackie discovered a new heroine: Madame de Récamier. She had lived in Paris in the early nineteenth century. She was beautiful, elegantly dressed, witty, and wealthy.

"Look at this portrait, Tuckie," said Jackie one afternoon. "She was painted by Jacques-Louis David, one of the best artists in Europe. All the most talented, brilliant, powerful people in France wanted to come to her salon."

Tuckie peered over Jackie's shoulder at the open art book on her desk. "Juliette de Récamier. That'll be you ten years from now, the Washington hostess with the mostest."

Jackie laughed. "*Quelle folie*—what foolishness! Nobody's even going to marry me. I'm certainly not going to marry any of those boys who step on my feet at dances."

Tuckie examined the portrait more closely. "No, I guess you're right. Madame de Récamier doesn't look like the type who'd try to show how sophisticated she was by smoking a cigarette during a movie, and cough so much that the usher made her leave the theater. Or the type who'd drop a piece of chocolate cream pie in a teacher's lap."

"But the pie was an accident!" Jackie's eyes widened in mock hurt. "You see, I am so *gauche,* so clumsy—I have not properly learned the deportment expected of a Miss Porter's girl."

"You're about as clumsy as a gazelle," said Tuckie with a snort. "And I heard Shella dare you to drop the pie when you served dessert."

Laughing, Jackie turned from the art book to the cookie tin. "Speaking of dessert—" She pried up the lid. "*Caramba!* The cookies are all gone. I guess it's time to make another Sunday evening raid on the pantry."

In the spring of 1947 Jackie graduated from Miss Porter's School. Her senior picture in the school yearbook showed her perfectly groomed, wearing a cashmere sweater and a single strand of pearls. The expression on her face was so poised, it was almost blank. None of the whimsical, mischievous Jackie showed through. But the ambition she'd given the yearbook hinted at a different Jackie: "Not to be a housewife."

Debutante of
the Year

Jackie stood next to blond Rosie Grosvenor, the other debutante of the evening, in the receiving line at the exclusive Clambake Club. The rooms were pine-paneled, the dance music polite. It was July 1947, and Jacqueline Bouvier was about to turn eighteen. Eighteen was the proper age for a young lady to be presented to society, according to the rules that were so important to Jackie's mother. And, as Janet Auchincloss often reminded Jackie, eighteen was also the proper age to start the search for a rich, socially acceptable husband.

"You could have worn my Dior gown," Janet had complained while Jackie was dressing for the party.

"Instead, you buy a dress off a department store rack for fifty-nine dollars!"

Jackie thought there were definitely some advantages for her in her mother's second marriage. Janet Auchincloss couldn't control her older daughter as well as she had when it was just Janet, Jackie, and Lee. Now Janet had two huge estates to run, as well as a family of seven children. Besides Jackie and Lee, there were Yusha from Hugh Auchincloss's first marriage, Nina and Tommy from his second marriage, little Janet, and now a new baby, James.

It was satisfying to go against Mummy's advice, especially since the mirror told Jackie she was right. The long white tulle off-the-shoulder dress she'd chosen was perfect. Together with her bouquet of red and white flowers, it set off her dark hair and her summer tan. Jackie smiled at her reflection, and her reflection gave her back a radiant smile. Why—she was *beautiful*.

A debutante party was a serious challenge—a challenge, in a way, like an important horse show. You had to look gorgeous. You had to dance with every single boy at the party. You had to make polite

chit-chat with each boy and his parents. You had to smile, smile, smile.

Jackie could play this game well, if she put her mind to it, just as she won prizes in the riding ring and earned top grades. Jackie had developed a soft, breathless voice that seemed to attract boys. When she fixed her wide, dark-lashed eyes on a boy and whispered, "Oh, I'm terrible at math too," the boy was enchanted. It never occurred to those boys to find out that Jackie's actual math grades were excellent.

At the same time, Jackie had no intention of giving up a good education. In the fall, she planned to go to college—not a finishing-school kind of college, but a serious women's college, Vassar. Mummy had encouraged Jackie to apply to Vassar. She wished she'd gone there instead of Sweet Briar in Virginia. And Daddy was happy about Vassar too. The college was in Poughkeepsie, New York, close enough to New York City for weekend visits with him.

Smiling sweetly at the next people in the reception line, Jackie offered a white-gloved hand. Smile, smile, smile. It was thrilling to be the belle of the ball, with all eyes on her. But this debutante in a white dress wasn't really Jackie. It was just a part that she played, like a role in a stage play. Inside, where no one at the party could see, was the real Jackie who studied history, adored the ballet, and read—even wrote!—poetry.

A few days after the debutante party, Jackie was off to Long Island and Lasata. She was worried about Danseuse, who wasn't well. Neither was Grampy Jack. Still, there was the usual big Bouvier family gathering on August 12, Grampy Jack's eighty-second birthday. Jackie read aloud a poem she'd written especially for him and decorated with drawings.

That fall, almost as soon as she'd unpacked her things at Vassar College, Jackie wanted to get away again. This small women's school, in its small town of Poughkeepsie on the Hudson River, seemed just as confining as Miss Porter's. Jackie made good grades, as usual, but she didn't stick around campus on the weekends. She went to football weekends at Yale, Harvard, or Princeton, or she visited her father in New York.

As it turned out, that birthday party at Lasata in the summer of 1947 was the last one. In January 1948 Jackie rode the train from Vassar to New York City. Grampy Jack had died, and his funeral would be held at St. Patrick's Cathedral in Manhattan.

Getting on the train at the Poughkeepsie station, Jackie noticed two college boys watching her walk down the aisle to take her seat. Now she heard them talking. She caught the phrase "Debutante of the Year."

Those stupid boys. Jackie had seen the society columns that came out at the end of the debutante season, but who cared what a gossip columnist said? "The No. 1 Deb of the Year—Jacqueline Bouvier, a regal brunette who has classic features and the daintiness of Dresden porcelain," gushed a columnist called "Cholly Knickerbocker." Jackie had made the Dean's List at Vassar last term, but nobody wrote *that* in a newspaper column.

At the funeral things were much worse than Jackie had expected. It was bad enough that Grampy Jack was dead. But besides that, everyone in the family was disappointed and angry.

All these years, the aunts and uncles and cousins had gathered summer after summer at Lasata, enjoying the gardens and orchards and stables and the lavish parties with well-trained servants. The family had assumed that Grampy Jack had plenty of money to pay for it all. He did not, as it turned out when the will was read. Grampy Jack had been spending money that his relatives expected to inherit.

"A nice legacy the old man left for his son and heir!" said Jack Bouvier that evening. He was tending bar as usual, pouring martinis for himself and his sisters. "What am I supposed to do with $100,000? I can't live on it."

"Don't forget your $50,000 loan, which he forgave," his sister Edith reminded him. "He gave me only $65,000, *total.* And the twins"—she shot a nasty look at Michelle and Maude—"cleaned up. *They* got Lasata."

"Lasata!" Michelle tossed her head. "As if we had the money to run Lasata. As if we could do anything with that white elephant except sell it, for half what it's worth."

The reign of Grampy Jack was over, thought Jackie. His kingdom was divided. There would be no more wonderful summers in East Hampton.

At the wake for John Vernou Bouvier Jr., throngs of mourners came to pay their respects. They brought expensive flower arrangements, which the aunts placed around the coffin. Jackie noticed an older man in a worn suit, someone she recognized. She used to see him working in the beautiful gardens at Lasata when she was a little girl.

The gardener offered one of the aunts a small bunch of violets. Taking the flowers impatiently, she stuck them into a larger bouquet.

That isn't right, thought Jackie. The gardener cared more about Grampy Jack than most of his so-called near and dear ones did. Rising from her seat, she pulled the violets from the bouquet and walked over to the open coffin.

Jackie knelt on the bench and tucked the violets down under her grandfather's elbow. Soon the coffin would be closed, and no one would notice the little bunch of flowers. "Goodbye, Grampy Jack," she whispered.

Riding the train back to Vassar College, Jackie felt the bleak January weather seeping into her. Grampy Jack was gone. He had left her and Lee only $3,000 apiece, to be put in trust accounts for them. Almost grown up, Jackie had no money of her own.

So many of the things Jackie loved—horses, beautiful clothes, summers on an elegant estate at the seashore—cost a lot of money. She couldn't expect her stepfather, Uncle Hughdie, to support her as if she were his own daughter. Daddy would love to give Jackie pots of money, if he had it—but he had barely enough for his little apartment in New York.

Jackie would have to take charge of her own future. No, there would be no more summers at Lasata. But there was another way for her to connect with the proud and elegant Bouvier family tradition. This summer, 1948, Jackie would find a way to go to Europe.

France, Land of "Our Forebears"

"If we go to one more museum," said Helen Bowdoin, a friend of Jackie's from Vassar, "my feet are going to drop off. Can't we just take a picture in front of the museum and then go sit in a cafe?"

"But this isn't just 'one more museum'—this is the Louvre," Miss Shearman, the chaperone, reminded her. "This is your chance to see some of the world's greatest art." Miss Shearman hadn't changed a bit since she was Jackie's Latin teacher at Holton-Arms School in Washington, D.C.

Jackie liked sitting in the sidewalk cafes in Paris as much as Helen did, and her feet ached from sightseeing too. But she'd spent the whole month of June studying up for this trip to Europe, and she wasn't going to miss a minute of it. High on her list of what she wanted to see was a particular painting in the Louvre.

Jackie and the three other girls in the group, all wearing the berets they had bought in Paris, followed their chaperone into the famous museum. Before long they stood in front of Jacques-Louis David's portrait of Jackie's heroine, Madame de Récamier. Jackie told her friends how all the famous politicians and writers and intellectuals in France had gathered at Juliette de Récamier's salon. "They knew they'd meet the most interesting people there—they'd have the most fascinating conversations," explained Jackie. "And her house was so beautiful and elegant."

"And *she* was beautiful," remarked Helen's sister, Judy. "She was awfully young, to be such a famous hostess." From the portrait Madame de Récamier smiled down at them. She seemed perfectly poised, although she was lounging on a chaise in a revealing Grecian gown.

Miss Shearman nodded approvingly at Jackie.

"What an excellent presentation, dear. We don't need a museum tour guide with you along."

During their stay in Paris, Jackie and her companions took a day trip to Versailles, palace of Louis XIV of France. Louis XIV, called the "Sun King" because of his brilliant reign, had knighted Grandfather Bouvier's ancestor de Vernou. Walking these elegant halls and formal gardens, Jackie felt almost dizzy with happiness. The other girls were ready to leave after a few hours, but at the end of the day Jackie was chatting with the guards in fluent French, asking questions about the palace.

"We have to leave *now*, Jackie," Helen informed her. "They close the gates in fifteen minutes. Do you want to spend the night at Versailles?"

"*Ah, oui*," breathed Jackie. "Oh, yes."

Before Paris, the group had already "done" London, including shaking hands with Sir Winston Churchill at a Buckingham Palace garden party. Now they raced on through France to the Riviera, then to Switzerland, and down the length of Italy to Florence and Rome.

On the first morning of their voyage homeward

on the *Queen Mary,* Helen flopped into a deck chair. "Hooray! No museums on board! No sights of any kind whatsoever. I may get up at lunchtime, and then again I may not."

Jackie stood at the deck railing, the salt breeze whipping her long curly hair. She had loved every hectic moment of the trip. Already she was planning how she could get back to France.

In the fall of 1948, Jackie wrote her mother and Uncle Hughdie that she was planning to spend her junior year abroad, in France. Vassar didn't have a junior year abroad program, but Jackie thought she could qualify for Smith College's program. When Jackie came home to Merrywood for Thanksgiving vacation, Janet and Hugh Auchincloss sat her down to discuss her plans.

Jackie could tell, even before her mother and stepfather started talking, that they didn't want her to spend a year in France. "Considerable additional expense," muttered Uncle Hughdie. For a multi-millionaire, thought Jackie, Uncle Hughdie could be very stingy.

"Yes," Janet agreed with her husband, "and

besides, France isn't the best place for you to meet the right sort of young man. You want to associate with men of substantial means who are well connected. Paris is full of long-haired bohemian types."

Paris is full of *interesting* types, thought Jackie. But she cast her eyes down and answered in a soft voice. "I know it would be an extra expense for me to live in Paris, and you're so generous already, Uncle Hughdie. Well, I've been thinking about another plan that I'd like almost as much. I could drop out of Vassar, move to New York City, and earn my own way as a fashion model. I could live with Daddy."

Janet gasped, and Jackie had to work hard not to smile.

"A fashion model!" said her mother. "That's not respectable work. I didn't go to all the trouble to bring you out in society to waste your chances like that! Get that notion out of your head right now."

"Maybe you're right," said Jackie. But her doubtful tone made it clear that she might do it anyway. That night, Janet and Hugh Auchincloss had a private talk about Jackie's future.

In the end, Hugh agreed to pay for Jackie's junior year in France. And a year later, in the fall of 1949, Jackie was in heaven—or, rather, Paris. She was studying at the Sorbonne, a section of the University of Paris founded in medieval times.

Jackie could have lived in a dormitory with other American students, but she was in France to live the French life. So Jackie rented a room from a landlady who spoke no English. This apartment on the avenue Mozart was so poorly heated that Jackie had to wear mittens while studying. There was only one little bathroom (often without hot water) for seven people. But Jackie loved it.

Jackie's landlady was the Comtesse Guyot de Renty, a dignified woman with white hair pulled back into a knot. Sitting at the dinner table with the Comtesse's family, Jackie listened to stories about her husband, the count. He had died working for the French Resistance during World War II. The countess herself had survived a concentration camp. Now she had to eke out a living by cooking for boarders—but she did it with style.

Besides Jackie's studies at the Sorbonne, she

took art lessons at the Louvre. She went to plays, to the ballet, to the opera. She strolled along the banks of the river Seine and sipped coffee in sidewalk cafes. She dated the son of a French diplomat.

At the end of that heavenly year, Jack Bouvier urged Jackie to go back to Vassar for her senior year of college. He'd get her a job on Wall Street after graduation, he promised. But Jackie's mother wanted Jackie nearby, and she certainly didn't want Jackie under her father's influence. She persuaded Jackie to transfer to Washington, D.C.

"You can commute to your classes from Merrywood, Janet pointed out. "And George Washington University has an outstanding French department."

George Washington University did have a good French department, and Jackie was just as glad to leave Vassar. The courses and teachers at Vassar were excellent, but a small girls' school was not for her. Also, Vassar was a long train ride from the city. There was a lot to be learned outside of classes, Jackie felt.

Jackie enjoyed going to her classes in French

language and history on the George Washington campus, just a few blocks from the White House. Still, she missed Paris. And she had an unsettled feeling. What was it, really, that she wanted to do with her life?

One day when Jackie came home to Merrywood from the city, Janet waved a clipping at her. "Look what I found in *Vogue* at the hairdresser. I think it would be great fun for you to enter this contest."

Dropping her books on a table, Jackie stood reading the clipping. Her breath shortened with excitement. The editors of the fashion magazine *Vogue* were announcing the annual Prix de Paris, a contest for young women in their last year of college. First prize was a job at *Vogue*—in the Paris office.

Jackie's Prize

Jackie threw herself into working on the contest application. It was a complicated, demanding task— just the kind of challenge Jackie relished. The first part was a personal essay describing herself.

Sitting cross-legged on the bed in her yellow bedroom at Merrywood, Jackie wrote and wrote. Usually Jackie was a very private person, but she told the contest judges about herself frankly. "I am tall, 5' 7", with brown hair, a square face, and eyes so unfortunately far apart that it takes three weeks to have a pair of glasses made with a bridge wide enough to fit over my nose. I do not have a sensational figure but can look slim if I pick the right clothes. I flatter myself on being able, at times, to walk out of the house looking like the poor man's Paris copy, but often my mother will run up to inform me that my left stocking seam is crooked or the right-hand topcoat button is about to fall off. This, I realize, is the Unforgivable Sin."

Jackie was also eager to tell *Vogue* why she wanted so much to go back to Paris. "Last winter I took my Junior Year in Paris. . . . I loved it more than any year of my life. . . . I learned not to be ashamed of a real hunger for knowledge, something I had always tried to hide."

Next, Jackie had to write an essay on "People I Wish I Had Known." Of course Jackie had been reading and thinking for years about remarkable people of the past. The difficult part was choosing only a few of them.

Finally Jackie decided on the French poet Charles Baudelaire, the author and playwright Oscar Wilde, and the ballet impresario Serge Diaghileff. These were all men who had devoted their lives to the arts. They were also people who had lived their personal lives with great flair, although not wisely. Baudelaire and Wilde were both rich men's sons who spent their inheritance recklessly and died poor.

Now came the technical parts of her application. *Vogue* wanted her to create a marketing campaign for a perfume, complete with a layout. They wanted her to discuss different methods of displaying new fashions in a magazine. And they asked her to design an entire imaginary issue of *Vogue*.

Jackie's application showed that she not only admired high fashion, but understood it thoroughly. Her mother and her father had both trained her to observe and criticize fashion. Janet had taught Jackie to strive for perfection in the way she dressed. Jack had taught Jackie to develop her own sense of style. Also, her years of drawing and painting and writing, on her own and for classes, gave her confidence in this work.

Thousands of college girls around the country read *Vogue,* and more than a thousand of them entered the Prix de Paris contest. But when the winners were notified in the spring of 1951, the first prize went to Jacqueline Bouvier. Her photograph would be featured in the August issue of *Vogue*, announcing the contest winners. And the editors of *Vogue* wanted Jackie to move to Paris and start work there as soon as she could.

Jackie was thrilled. She imagined herself swishing into Paris night clubs, climbing the marble staircase of the Opera, or pausing at a bookstall along the Seine, always in elegant outfits. She, Jackie, would help shape the world of high fashion!

However, her mother was not thrilled, in spite of the fact that the contest had been her idea. One evening they had a long discussion in Janet's dressing room, as Jackie's mother was getting ready to go out.

"Of course the Prix de Paris is quite an honor, Jacqueline, but I wouldn't let it go to your head." Leaning toward her dressing table mirror, Janet applied eyebrow pencil with deft strokes. "Think how young and inexperienced you are. There's quite a difference between living in Paris as a student and putting yourself up against the top professionals in the fashion world. I don't want to let you get into a situation where you're bound to embarrass yourself."

Jackie had felt on top of the world when she first got the letter from *Vogue*. But now her confidence was draining away. Probably Mummy was right. Those super-talented, super-competent fashion people would chew her up and spit her out. The judges of the Prix de Paris would soon realize what a mistake they'd made in choosing her.

"Not only that," Janet went on, spraying perfume first on one side of her throat, then the other. "I'm also concerned about your future security. You're twenty-two now, almost twenty-three. Many of your classmates from Miss Porter's are married—*well* married. Why, I was only twenty-one when I married your father."

And look how that turned out, thought Jackie. Still, her mother's words sank in. To her friends, Jackie might say flip things about how she'd never marry. "I'll end up as a housemother at Miss Porter's School," she'd joked to Tuckie. But inside, she shuddered at the idea.

Janet seemed to sense that Jackie was weakening. She gave her a bright smile from the mirror. "Darling, Uncle Hughdie and I have a surprise for you and Lee. To celebrate Lee's graduation from Miss Porter's and your graduation from college, we want to send you both to Europe for the summer."

"But *Vogue* wants me to start work at their Paris office this summer," protested Jackie.

"An office full of *women*," said her mother. Jackie understood quite well what Janet meant: An office full of women was no place to meet her future husband.

"Of course we'll give you and Lee introductions to all the right people in London and Paris and Italy," continued Janet. "How would you like to meet the art critic Bernard Berenson, for instance? He lives in Florence."

"Bernard Berenson," gasped Jackie. She wanted very much to meet him. And she had to admit that she didn't want to end up unmarried, pinching and scrimping to live on a tiny income. In the end, Jackie turned down the *Vogue* prize that she and more than a thousand other young women had wanted so badly.

Instead, Jackie went off to Europe with Lee, and the summer of 1951 was a great fling for both of them. Buying a car in England, the sisters toured merrily around the Continent. They danced, they flirted, and they saw the finest paintings and statues and buildings in Europe. In Italy they visited the famous art critic Bernard Berenson. He gave them some advice that deeply impressed Jackie: "The only way to exist happily is to love your work."

Jackie felt that this must be true, but she didn't understand how it could apply to *her* life. What was her work? It couldn't mean having a career. Jackie had to get married, and no worthwhile husband would want his wife to have a career.

Returning home, Jackie and Lee wrote and illustrated a handmade book about their adventures and presented it to their mother. They'd pasted in a picture of the two of them in a public square in Rome, Lee dressed in shorts and Jackie in tight pants and sandals. The teasing caption said, "We never do anything that would call attention to us and make people shocked at Americans. We . . . never go out in big cities except in what we would wear to church in Newport on Sundays."

But now the summer of fun was over, and Jackie

felt more unsettled than before about what to do with her life. What she instinctively wanted to do was all wrong, it seemed. She longed to live in Paris, and she'd been thrilled and proud at the prospect of working for a top fashion magazine. As for a future husband, the most likely prospect seemed to be John Husted, a young man she was dating. Jackie didn't find him very exciting, but at this point she didn't trust her own feelings.

At first Janet encouraged the match with John Husted, the son of friends of the Auchinclosses. But by the time he proposed to Jackie in December of 1951, Janet had discovered that John didn't have any money except what he earned as an investment banker. "That is not *real* money," Janet told Jackie one morning. As she talked, Janet was inspecting a box of imported Irish crystal that had just been delivered to Merrywood.

"But John and I love each other!" said Jackie—although privately, she wasn't so sure. "Shouldn't that be enough?"

Janet gave a scornful sniff. "Jacqueline. Do you remember what you wrote for the yearbook, your last year at Miss Porter's? You said your goal was 'not to be a housewife.' Well, you're heading straight for a life of housewifery. If you marry John, do you really think you'll have a country estate with a stable? Do you think you'll be able to travel, or to choose nice things like *this*?" She held a cut-glass goblet up to the light.

"I'm twenty-three, Mummy." Jackie's voice trembled with anger. For one moment she felt it would be worth wearing a housewife's apron and doing her own cooking and cleaning, just to spite her mother. "You can't tell me who I can see and who I can't."

But a month or so later, Jackie broke off her engagement with John Husted and began dating other men. One of those men was a congressman from Massachusetts named John F. Kennedy. Jackie had met him the year before, and she was intrigued.

Jack Kennedy was a tall, lean man of thirty-four with a boyish grin that made him look much younger. His sense of humor matched Jackie's own. She admired him for the courage he'd shown in the Navy in World War II. She was impressed that he made light of the pain he still suffered from his battle wounds.

Jack was from a big Irish family—an immensely wealthy family. Talk about *real* money! Jack's personal trust fund alone was $10 million.

On the minus side—in Jackie's view—Jack was allergic to horses and dogs. He wasn't very romantic. He traveled a lot for his work in politics. And most discouraging, he didn't seem eager to get married.

Or did he? It was confusing. In the summer of 1952, Jack invited Jackie to the Kennedy resort at Hyannis Port, on Cape Cod, Massachusetts, to meet his family. He was seen with her so much that by November 1952, when he was elected to the Senate, rumors were flying around Washington that they were almost engaged. In January 1953, Jack took Jackie to the very public, very political event of President Eisenhower's inauguration. The next month, Jackie introduced Jack Kennedy to her father in New York, and the young Democrat Jack went out of his way to make friends with the older Republican Jack.

All during this time Jackie kept on living at Merrywood. She couldn't afford to pay rent for an apartment, although she had a job. She worked for the *Washington Times-Herald* as "inquiring photographer." Her job was to think up interesting questions to ask people on the street, take their pictures, and write up a column for the newspaper.

In the spring of 1953 the inquiring photographer went to Capitol Hill to interview senators and their pages, the boys who ran errands and delivered messages. She also interviewed Vice President Richard M. Nixon. Nixon had been a senator from California before he and Dwight D. Eisenhower were elected in 1952. To Jackie's questions about the pages, the vice president answered in his deep, impressive voice, "I would predict that some future statesman will come from the ranks of the page corps."

Jackie had more fun interviewing Senator John F. Kennedy. Although she'd been dating him for more than a year, she put on her best professional journalist manner with him.

"Can you stand over there, Senator?" asked Jackie in her soft, breathless voice. "Yes, beside the flag."

She raised the heavy Speed Flash Graflex camera used by news photographers. "What is it like to observe the Senate pages at close range?"

Jack pretended to consider the question carefully. "I've often thought that the country might be better off if we Senators and the pages traded jobs."

"I'm going to quote you, Senator," Jackie warned him.

"I'm going to take you to dinner tomorrow night," Jack shot back.

"Tomorrow?" Jackie tucked her camera into her carryall bag. "Oh, I'd *love* to—but I'm busy tomorrow night." She gave him a dazzling smile. "Thank you so much for the interview, Senator. Goodbye."

Not long after that, Jackie had a thrilling opportunity. If she wanted, she could go to London and cover the coronation of Queen Elizabeth II for the *Washington Times-Herald*. It was a reporter's chance of a lifetime. And it would show Jack Kennedy that she wasn't sitting around, waiting for him to decide if he really wanted to marry her.

That May, Jacqueline Bouvier's stories and sketches of the coronation events appeared on the front page of the *Times-Herald*. When she returned to the United States, Jack Kennedy was waiting for her at the airport. There was a diamond and emerald engagement ring in his pocket.

Becoming a Kennedy

The Fourth of July was a big gathering time for the Kennedys. Joe Kennedy, Jack's father, brought them all together in Hyannis Port. The Kennedy "compound," as they called it, was a cluster of houses on the waterfront.

Jack's father and mother, Joe and Rose Kennedy, stayed in the Cape Cod–style "big house." There was plenty of room in the other houses for Jack's six brothers and sisters and their wives or husbands, children, and friends. But the noisy, active Kennedy clan seemed to take up more room than normal people, thought Jackie. This Fourth of July, 1953, was her second Independence Day with the

Kennedys, so she knew what to expect.

The Kennedys' idea of a relaxing weekend was sports, sports, and more sports. The tennis matches and sailing races in the afternoon weren't so bad, but Jackie hated the mornings of touch football. "I guess debutantes don't play football," Jack's sister Eunice teased Jackie. The Kennedys had already teased her about her chic clothes, her whispery voice, and about speaking French with another family friend. To be a good sport, Jackie gritted her teeth and played football.

Jackie wasn't weak or timid, but she'd been brought up to compete fiercely while remaining graceful and ladylike. The Kennedy sisters had been brought up to join in the free-for-all with their brothers. Ethel, Robert's wife, was just as bad. These "rah-rah girls," as Jackie secretly called them, still played touch football with gusto, even if they were pregnant.

This morning Jackie said sweetly, "I'll just sit over here in the shade and talk to Joe." She smiled at her father-in-law to be, and he smiled back. They'd hit it off the first time they met.

110

Jackie knew that Joe Kennedy had had something to do with the emerald and diamond engagement ring on her left hand. Joseph P. Kennedy was the ruler of the extended Kennedy family, even more than Grampy Jack had been the ruler of the Bouviers. Joe was determined that his eldest son would go into politics—and become the first Irish-Catholic president of the United States. After his first son, Joe Kennedy Jr., had been killed in World War II, he expected Jack to fill that role.

The previous Fourth-of-July weekend, Joe had privately told his son Jack it was high time for him to get married. Looking ahead to the election of 1960, Jack planned to run for president. But as they both knew, an unmarried man had no chance of being elected to the presidency.

Furthermore, said Joe, Jack's wife should be classy, which the rough-and-tumble Irish Kennedys were certainly not. Jack's sisters, Eunice and Kathleen, might make fun of Jackie's cultivated manners and Miss Porter's School style. Joe, however, thought she was exactly the wife that Senator John F. Kennedy needed at his side when he ran for the highest office in the land. Jack's mother agreed.

Now Jack and Jackie's wedding date was set for September 12. Janet Auchincloss, who had just planned and brought off Lee's wedding that spring, envisioned another wedding in perfect good taste and style. Joe Kennedy, on the other hand, saw the wedding as a wonderful chance to launch his son toward the presidency.

To get the full publicity benefit out of the wedding, Joe insisted on inviting hundreds of people who weren't exactly relatives or friends. They were people who could help Jack get elected president.

"Journalists! Hollywood celebrities! Politicians!" Janet moaned to Jackie, pointing to a list that Jack's secretary had sent. "He's trying to turn our wedding into a vulgar circus. What will our friends think?"

Jackie didn't especially want a vulgar circus either. Sometimes, when she thought about becoming a Kennedy, she felt panicky. Would her life from now on be an endless Kennedy touch football game, shouting and crowding and jostling and fighting to win, win, *win?*

Still, Jackie had to laugh, seeing her strong-willed mother struggling against the stronger will of Joe Kennedy. Janet came up with what she thought was the perfect excuse: The Auchinclosses shouldn't have to pay for all the Kennedys' extra guests. Joe promptly agreed to pay—and that was the end of that argument.

Joe wanted a say about every detail of the wedding, including the bride's dress. Jackie had developed her own personal style, influenced by Paris designs. She knew that what suited her best were slim dresses with simple lines. But Joe was determined that Jackie's wedding dress would be ultra-traditional. He won, and Jackie wore a dress made of fifty yards of cream-colored silk faille, with rows and rows of ruffles in the full skirt. "It looked a little like a lampshade," said Jackie later.

Janet and Joe disagreed about many things, but they were both worried that Jack Bouvier might ruin the wedding. They deliberately left him out of all the parties before the wedding, and they hoped to leave him out of the wedding ceremony itself. Traditionally, the father of the bride walks the bride down the aisle of the church. But could Jackie's father be trusted to stay sober? True, he had walked Lee down the aisle just fine last spring, but so much more depended on his performance at Jackie's wedding. Maybe sober, reliable Hugh Auchincloss should stand in for him.

Jackie wanted to please her mother and future father-in-law, but she insisted on having her own father give her away. She was willing to smile and shake hands with hundreds and hundreds of strangers at the reception. She was willing to look like a lampshade on the most important day of her life. But she was *not* willing to shut her beloved father out of her wedding party.

September 12, 1953, was a bright, breezy wedding day for Senator John Fitzgerald Kennedy and Jacqueline Lee Bouvier. Eight hundred guests filled St. Mary's Church in Newport, Rhode Island. Archbishop Cushing of Boston was there to perform the ceremony. Outside the church, more than three thousand curious onlookers waited to catch a glimpse of the bride. But Jack Bouvier, drinking heavily in his hotel room, did not show up. "I'm not surprised," said Janet to her daughter. "Uncle Hughdie will walk you down the aisle."

With the poise and self-control she'd learned at the Chapin School and Miss Porter's, Jackie got through the ceremony. On the church steps afterward, she managed big smiles for the newspaper photographers waiting outside. The newspaper stories the next day noted Jackie's delicate lace veil, the same one Janet's mother had worn as a bride. Lee had also worn it in her wedding that April. The newspapers described Jackie's bouquet of orchids, gardenias, and stephanotis. No one seemed to notice her swollen eyes.

Back at Hammersmith Farm, Jackie had a few private moments in her room to cry again with her sister. "Oh, Lee," she sobbed. "Daddy stayed sober long enough to give you away. Why couldn't he do this for me?"

Lee didn't realize, any more than Jackie did, how insulted and hurt their father had been at the way the Auchinclosses and Kennedys left him out of the celebrations. She didn't have an answer. But she brought Jackie a cold washcloth for her reddened eyes, and she helped her repair her makeup. Then the bride and her matron of honor went downstairs to face the audience and the cameras again.

It took more than two hours for all the guests to go through the receiving line. Jackie overheard a woman she'd seen in London last spring gushing to another guest, "This is just like the coronation!" Jackie posed for photograph after photograph. There were pictures of Jackie and Jack cutting the cake; Jackie and Jack on the beautifully groomed lawns of Hammersmith Farm with the wedding party of ten bridesmaids and fourteen ushers; Jackie throwing her bouquet from the top of the staircase. These pictures weren't just for the family album—they would appear in newspapers all over the country.

For the next several years Senator and Mrs. John F. Kennedy lived in rented houses in Washington, D.C. Jackie took up the role of a senator's wife, which in those days meant taking care of her husband and socializing to help his political career. She was expected, for instance, to attend many

teas and luncheons for Senate wives. Most of the other women at these events were Jackie's mother's age, and she was bored silly.

Jackie was not naturally interested in politics—in fact, she had never even voted. But now she began reading the *Congressional Record,* she attended all Jack's speeches in the Senate, and she studied American history at Georgetown University. Jackie also put her knowledge of French to Jack's use, translating official reports and conversations for him.

Jackie did enjoy pampering Jack, who was careless about his health and his personal appearance. She chose suits and ties for him. She brought gourmet lunches to his Senate office to replace the peanut butter sandwiches he'd eat at his desk.

But these activities didn't add up to a satisfying way of life for Jackie. She missed Jack terribly when he was traveling, which was much of the time. Jackie filled in her days with decorating and redecorating her house or shopping for clothes.

In spite of his youthful appearance, Jack Kennedy was not in good health. He suffered from Addison's disease, a serious illness that had damaged his immune system. Even a cold was dangerous for him, and any wound was slow to heal. His back pain became so bad that he had to use crutches.

In spite of the risk, Jack decided to have an operation on his back. In 1954 he underwent complicated surgery. Jackie was afraid he would die— and he nearly did. While Jack was in bed for months afterward, Jackie spent all her time at his side. She not only kept him company, but she calmly changed the bandages on his wound.

The first operation was unsuccessful. In 1955 Jack had more back surgery, followed by several months of recovery. During that time he worked on his book *Profiles in Courage*. It was about U. S. senators who had taken a serious political risk for something they thought was right. Jackie also worked on the book, as Jack acknowledged in his preface. She helped do the research, she read her findings to Jack, and she edited the manuscript. The next year, the book won the prestigious Pulitzer Prize for biography.

Jackie's father was not well either. A lifetime of

hard drinking caught up with him, and in August 1957 Jack Bouvier died of liver cancer. Jackie was glad that at least her father and her husband had gotten to know each other. They had enjoyed each other's company, in spite of their political differences.

Meanwhile, Jackie had her own health problems. She and Jack were eager to have children, but her first pregnancy miscarried, and so did her second. Finally, on the day before Thanksgiving 1957, Jack and Jackie's first healthy baby, Caroline, was born. "This is the happiest day of my life," Jackie told Jack.

In 1958 Jack ran for reelection to the senate. Jackie left Caroline with their nanny, Maud Shaw, and campaigned for her husband. The whole Kennedy clan campaigned. Jack won by a wide margin, but that was just a warm-up campaign for the presidential election of 1960.

The expression "running for office," Jackie thought, seemed to have been invented especially for Jack. He was always literally dashing out the door to catch a plane to somewhere or other.

Jackie had never loved politics, and she disliked them now more than ever. She wanted to be home with three-year-old Caroline, and she thought Jack should be there too.

Putting aside her feelings, Jackie toured the country with Jack, appearing with him and sometimes filling in for him at campaign stops. She shook hands and smiled until she thought her right hand would drop off and her face would freeze. In one supermarket in Wisconsin, she charmed the manager into giving her the microphone and urged the surprised shoppers to vote for "my husband, John F. Kennedy." She delighted voters in ethnic neighborhoods by giving talks in fluent French or Italian or Spanish. She also did a television advertisement in Spanish, which was very unusual at the time.

Young, stylish Jackie got more attention than she wanted from reporters. They jumped on every detail (true or not) that they could dig up about her personal life. Had she really spent $30,000 on clothes in 1960? asked a reporter from the *New York Times*. "I couldn't spend that much unless I wore sable underwear," snapped Jackie. Jack's campaign was not pleased when the *Times* printed her answer on page one. And Jackie began to realize how hard she would have to fight now to keep her private life private.

During the summer of 1960 Jackie dropped out of the campaign because she was pregnant again. She would do almost anything for her husband, but she would not risk losing the baby. In July she and little Caroline cheered for Jack from Hyannis Port when he won the Democratic nomination. Janet and Hugh Auchincloss were there cheering too. Although they had always been firmly Republican, they were proud of their son-in-law and supported his run for the presidency.

In September, when Jack debated Republican candidate Richard Nixon, Jackie watched the debate on television. However, Jackie herself was shown on TV, sitting in her living room. Off-camera, the room was crammed with reporters and photographers.

On Tuesday, November 8, Jack and Jackie voted and then awaited the election results at Hyannis

Port. The election results were very close. It was Wednesday morning before the Kennedys, the nation, and the world were sure that John F. Kennedy would become the thirty-fifth president of the United States. While the Kennedy clan and friends at the compound celebrated in noisy Kennedy style, Jackie went off by herself for a walk on the beach. A few days later, she told a reporter from *Time* magazine, "I feel as though I have just turned into a piece of public property."

On November 25, 1960, John Fitzgerald Kennedy Jr., was born. Jack and Jackie were relieved and delighted, of course, but the whole nation was thrilled. For the first time since 1893, there would be a First Baby in the White House.

Queen Jacqueline

The morning of Inauguration Day, January 20, 1961, was bitterly cold in Washington, D.C. Eight inches of snow had fallen the day before, and now the thermometer stayed well below freezing. Still, crowds turned out in Washington to see the inauguration. People were excited about the Kennedys, a glamorous young couple, especially in contrast to the Eisenhowers. President Dwight Eisenhower had been the oldest president so far, and John F. Kennedy would be the youngest. Millions of viewers were also watching the inauguration on television.

Jackie was keenly aware of all those eyes

watching. Only two months before, she had suffered a difficult childbirth by Caesarian section, and she was still recovering. But she stood beside her husband on the steps of the Capitol as he was sworn in. She listened proudly to his inaugural speech, with its idealistic call to action: "Ask not what your country can do for you: Ask what you can do for your country."

Jackie understood how important it was for her to be there that day—and to be standing straight, smiling her radiant smile, and looking smashing. Her outfit, a beige wool coat with a sable collar and a beige pillbox hat, had been created especially for her by the fashion designer Oleg Cassini. Cassini had also designed her white satin and chiffon gown for the inaugural ball.

Between Election Day and Inauguration Day, Jackie had visited the White House for the customary tour. Republican Mamie Eisenhower, the First Lady, had not been especially welcoming. Jackie was still exhausted and weak from the difficult birth of John F. Kennedy Jr.

And the White House itself looked even worse

than Jackie remembered from her tour many years before. Afterward she moaned to her secretary, "It's the worst place in the world! So cold and dreary . . ." She added the most biting insult she could think of: "It looks like it's been furnished by discount stores."

On Inauguration Day, after the swearing-in ceremony, there was a reception at the White House for family members. With all the Bouvier clan and all the Kennedy clan, there were about 130 guests. Jackie, after her brave public appearance at the inauguration, went upstairs to lie down. She knew the relatives would be disappointed not to be greeted personally by her. At the same time, she doubted she could make it to the inaugural ball that evening if she didn't get some rest. Downstairs, her mother took over as hostess and saw to it that everyone was welcomed and introduced.

On her first day as First Lady, Jackie was figuring out how much of her role she was able and willing to fill. She wasn't enthusiastic about the very term "First Lady." Shortly after the Kennedys moved into the White House, she told the Chief Usher, J.B. West, "The one thing I do not want to be called is 'First Lady.' It sounds like a saddle horse."

On the other hand, being the president's wife was the opportunity of a lifetime. Jackie realized that, and she had ideas about how she would use her opportunity. First of all, she would make the White House a place Americans could be proud of.

Many First Ladies in the past had redecorated the White House to their own taste, but Jackie had something different in mind. The White House, she thought, ought to reflect periods of American history. As she explained to Jack, "It looks like a place where nothing has ever taken place." She was horrified to find imitation Louis XV furniture in the Red Room. Not only was the furniture tacky-looking, but it imitated a historical period *before* the existence of the White House or even the existence of the United States of America!

Instead of merely redecorating, Jackie intended to *restore* the White House. She would give its history back to the American people. She would make the president's house historically accurate *and* elegant—an inspiration to everyone who visited.

Jackie threw herself into her special project. Art and history had always been favorite subjects of hers, and now she focused intently on White House architecture and the history of American interior design. She contacted experts in art and antiques, as well as people who could help her raise money. She met with the chairman of the Commission of Fine Arts and the director of the National Gallery. And she personally grubbed around in the basement and warehouses of the White House to find neglected historic pieces.

Jackie tracked down pieces of furniture and furnishings, such as Thomas Jefferson's inkstand, that had once belonged to the White House. The people who now owned these items found out how hard it was to say no to Jackie Kennedy. She had a soft, flattering way of asking, but she usually got what she wanted. "If you have a bed that used to be in the White House," one committee member complained, "she'll have you sleeping on the floor before you know what happened."

Jackie also had the idea for a historic guide to the White House, the kind of guide she'd wished for when she visited Washington at age eleven. Jackie supervised the writing, edited the guide, and wrote an introduction to it. Published on July 4, 1962, *The White House: An Historic Guide* was an immediate best-seller. The money it earned was used to pay for historic furnishings for the White House.

Earlier that year, in February 1962, the whole country had the chance to see what Jacqueline Kennedy had achieved. In a television special, "A Tour of the White House with Mrs. John F. Kennedy," she showed the American people *their* White House. Over forty-eight million viewers watched her point out such national treasures as Dolley Madison's sofa in the Red Room. She was especially proud of the Diplomatic Reception Room with its antique wallpaper, a panorama of early nineteenth-century American scenes.

Jackie lavished care on the private quarters at the White House too. She wanted her home to be beautiful, but comfortable and inviting. In the

solarium, a large, sunny room on the third floor of the White House, she set up a nursery school. Here Caroline and John could spend time with boys and girls their own age, children of friends and staff members. There were two teachers, but Jackie and the other mothers also took turns reading stories to the children, playing games, and singing songs with them.

Jackie also arranged schedules so that Jack could have lunch every day with his wife and children. He needed the time for relaxation, and his children needed to see him. Before the election, an interviewer had asked Jackie what the major role of the First Lady should be. "To take care of the President, so he can best serve the people," Jackie had answered.

But her children came first. "If you bungle raising your children," she said, "I don't think whatever else you do well matters very much." Of course Jackie's idea of raising children included their nanny, Maud Shaw, who looked after them much of the time.

Meanwhile, the "Jackie look" swept the nation.

Women all over the country wore pillbox hats and sleeveless sheath dresses like Jackie's. They wore their hair in Jackie's bouffant style. Jackie, with the help of designer Oleg Cassini, had a much bigger impact on fashion then she ever could have if she'd become an editor at *Vogue*.

With her soft voice and demure manner, Jackie often fooled people into thinking that there was nothing much going on underneath her bouffant hairdo. Jack Kennedy, however, knew his wife better than that. As time went on, the president realized that Jackie was a tremendous asset to his work.

In 1961 President Kennedy and his wife made an official trip to Europe. The first stop was Paris, where Jackie was thrilled to be welcomed by French President Charles de Gaulle. During World War II, he'd been her hero, and she'd even named her dog "Gaullie" after him. Now it was de Gaulle's turn to be impressed by Jackie. Her bearing was regal, her wide-eyed gaze fascinating. Also, this *américaine* spoke fluent French, and she knew French history— more than any Frenchwoman, de Gaulle declared.

A high point of the visit was the formal state

dinner at the palace of Versailles. Thirteen years before, Jackie had wandered the halls of Versailles as an awestruck tourist. Now she was an honored guest, the American queen. At least Jackie looked like a queen in her designer gown. It was white satin, studded with rhinestones, with a red-white-and-blue bodice. She even wore a diamond tiara.

The whole French nation seemed to fall wildly in love with Jackie. Wherever she went in France, crowds appeared. "Jacqui! Jacqui!" they chanted. President Kennedy, in his speech to the Paris Press Club, joked that he was "the man who accompanied Jacqueline Kennedy to Paris."

Back in Washington, Jackie worked to bring the best of everything to the White House. The president and his wife should set a high cultural standard for the country, she felt. In France, the arts were honored and celebrated—why not in America?

So Jackie invited world-famous artists to perform for the president and his guests. Ballets and Shakespeare plays were staged in the East Room, the largest state reception room. Musicians such as the brilliant cellist Pablo Casals played at the White

House. Artists and writers were often among the guests at Jackie's elegant White House dinners. Like Madame de Récamier, Jackie wanted to entertain the most accomplished, the wittiest, the most exciting people in the country—in the *world*.

When the president of Pakistan, Ayub Khan, visited Washington in 1961, Jackie put on an especially glamorous dinner in his honor. The 150 guests were ferried up the Potomac and then driven in limousines to Mt. Vernon, George Washington's home. The National Symphony Orchéstra played as the guests drank mint juleps on the portico and then dined in beautifully decorated tents.

While Jackie had a strong sense of her role as the President's wife, she didn't necessarily agree with what other people (including her husband) thought that role should be. Sometimes she simply refused to perform the duties that First Ladies like Mamie Eisenhower had always done so faithfully. Receptions, teas, luncheons with congressional wives or clubwomen bored Jackie silly, and often she didn't show up for these events. Lady Bird Johnson, the vice-president's wife, or Jackie's mother would have to act as hostess instead. They made excuses for Jackie, but it would come out later that the First Lady had been riding in the country or watching the London Royal Ballet.

It wasn't easy for Jackie to keep any private life when the public wanted to know all about her, and reporters and photographers watched her every move. Eleanor Roosevelt, President Roosevelt's widow, had warned Jackie that living in the White House would be like living in a goldfish bowl. It was true.

Journalists spied on the First Lady with binoculars, pried information out of the White House maids, and lay in wait for Jackie wherever she went. It became more important than ever to have people around her she could trust, and she was glad to have her old friend Nancy Tuckerman for her social secretary. When one interviewer asked Jackie what her German shepherd puppy liked to eat, she answered, "Reporters."

The End of Camelot

Since 1949 the United States had been locked in a nuclear arms race with the Soviet Union. By the time President Kennedy took office, the United States and Russia together had enough nuclear weapons to destroy civilization. In October 1962 Americans learned that the Soviet Union was placing nuclear missiles at a base in Cuba, only ninety miles from Florida. President Kennedy sent the U.S. Navy to blockade Cuba. He demanded that Soviet leader Nikita Khruschev withdraw the missiles, and he announced that the United States would attack Russia if any of the Cuban missiles were used.

There was a danger that the Soviet Union would attack Washington. In fact, a full-scale nuclear war could break out. If this happened, Washington, D.C., and the state of Virginia, at the least, would be wiped out. At the worst, a nuclear war could end life on Earth.

Jack asked Jackie to take Caroline and John to a place near their underground bomb shelter, but Jackie refused. She would stay with her husband, no matter what happened. Luckily Khruschev backed down and removed the missiles, and the Cuban missile crisis was resolved.

In August of 1963 the Kennedys suffered a personal tragedy. That spring, Jackie had been delighted to be pregnant again. The public was delighted too, to look forward to a new baby in the White House. This would be the first baby born to a sitting president since Frances and Grover Cleveland's third daughter was born in 1893.

Sadly, the Kennedys' baby, Patrick, did not survive. He was born prematurely, struggling to breathe. He lived less than two days.

Sometimes the terrible strain of the death of a

child can break up a marriage. But for the Kennedys, losing Patrick seemed to draw them closer together. Jack was more tender and attentive with Jackie. For her part, Jackie wanted to be more help to him in his work. "I'll campaign with you anywhere you want," she told Jack. That November, when he flew to Texas on an important political trip, she went along.

President Kennedy was not well liked in Texas—to put it mildly. He was a liberal Massachusetts Catholic, while most Texans were conservative Protestants. In 1960 John F. Kennedy had chosen Lyndon Johnson for his vice president partly to get the Southern Democrat vote. Now the president was beginning to run for reelection in 1964, and he would need Southern votes again.

To Jackie's surprise, she actually enjoyed the trip to Texas. The stops in San Antonio, Houston, and Fort Worth were not so bad. Maybe she was having a good time because Jack seemed to appreciate her support more than ever before.

For the appearance in Dallas, Jackie dressed in her bright pink wool suit, as Jack asked her to.

They drove through the city in a motorcade in the presidential car, a Lincoln convertible with a bubble top. Jack insisted on having the top of the car removed so that there was nothing between President and Mrs. Kennedy and the cheering crowds along the streets.

The afternoon was hot, and the sun was blinding. Jackie was uncomfortable in her wool suit, but she smiled and waved, waved and smiled. As the car rolled on past throngs of enthusiastic Texans, Jackie noticed a tunnel ahead. It will be cooler in the tunnel, she thought.

Suddenly, three shots rang out. John F. Kennedy, thirty-fifth President of the United States, died almost immediately from wounds to his head. An assassin, Lee Harvey Oswald, had fired his rifle from the window of a building along the motorcade route.

The next few hours were a hideous nightmare for Jackie. Stunned and distraught, she hardly knew what she was saying or doing. But by the time she and Vice President and Mrs. Johnson were on board Air Force One, bringing the president's body back to Washington, she was considering what she could do.

Her first act was to support the new President of the United States. During the flight from Dallas to Washington, Lyndon Johnson was sworn in. His wife, Lady Bird, stood on one side of him, and Jacqueline Kennedy stood on the other. She refused to change her bloodstained pink suit for the ceremony. "Let them see what they have done," she said.

Jackie knew that in 1865, when President Abraham Lincoln was assassinated, Mary Lincoln had collapsed. She was not even able to attend the funeral. But Jackie Kennedy was a stronger woman. She understood well that being queen didn't only mean waving to admiring crowds. In a time of national tragedy, the queen could not fall apart. She was needed to lead the nation in mourning.

As stoic as a soldier, Jackie planned her husband's state funeral at St. Matthew's Cathedral in Washington. It would be modeled on President Lincoln's funeral, to emphasize the historical connection. In the funeral procession from the White

House to St. Matthew's Cathedral, one riderless horse was led behind the horse-drawn caisson with the coffin, to show that the country's leader was missing. Jackie herself, dignified and regal in a black veil, marched behind her husband's flag-draped coffin.

Caroline was not quite six, and John not quite three years old. Their nanny had told them that their father had been shot, and they felt the anguish of all the adults around them. But Jackie expected her children to rise to this occasion, just as she did. At the right moment in the ceremonies Jackie whispered to John, and he stepped forward and saluted his father's coffin.

The Kennedy family wanted Jack to be buried in Boston, his home town. But Jackie decided that he should be buried at Arlington National Cemetery, that peaceful place she had first seen at the age of twelve. It was fitting, she felt, that a slain president should rest on a hill overlooking the nation's capital.

Jackie also decided that an eternal flame, like the flame ever burning at the Tomb of the Unknown

Soldier in Paris, would burn beside her husband's grave. At the burial, she lighted the taper to light the flame. Afterward, she returned to the White House and received all the foreign leaders who had come to pay their respects.

Clearly Jackie had asked herself, just as President Kennedy had urged in his inauguration speech, what she could do for her country. She led the nation in mourning its slain president with dignity and style. As French President Charles de Gaulle put it, "She gave the world an example of how to behave."

However, Jackie put up a wall, as she always had, between the family's public duty and their private life. The night after Jack's burial, Jackie went ahead with the birthday party she'd planned for John. And two days after that, they celebrated Caroline's birthday.

Jackie also had strong ideas about the way she wanted her husband to be remembered. She wanted history to remember the way he had lived, not just the horrible way he had died. At Hyannis Port, a week after Jack's death, she explained her thoughts to journalist Theodore H. White.

To sum up her ideas, Jackie quoted a song from the musical *Camelot*. This musical, a major Broadway hit, was based on the legend of King Arthur and his court. Both Jack and Jackie, as children, had been enthralled by the stories about King Arthur.

Now one particular line in the song "Camelot" seemed to say what Jackie was feeling: "Don't let it be forgot, that once there was a spot, for one brief, shining moment that was known as Camelot." She wanted John F. Kennedy's presidency to be remembered as a time of high ideals and heroes, like King Arthur's Knights of the Round Table.

Theodore White wrote about Jackie's "Camelot" idea in a lead article for *Life* magazine. The idea caught on immediately, as others who admired and grieved for President Kennedy sought to express what they had lost. Others scoffed at the "Camelot" idea, saying that unsentimental Jack Kennedy himself would have made fun of it. But for many people, there will always be the glow of a noble myth over that time in American history.

✹ ✹ ✹

Jackie was now a private person—or so she thought. She'd done her duty by the American people, painful as it was. With Nancy Tuckerman's help, she'd answered nearly 800,000 letters of sympathy. In January 1964, Jackie appeared on television to thank the letter writers. Those letters, she said, would be saved at the John F. Kennedy Library to be built in Boston.

Now Jackie expected to drop out of public life and live her private life as she thought best. But the public still considered Jackie Kennedy its property. Tourist buses stopped right in front of her house in Georgetown, D.C., to point out where she and her children lived. Some fans tried to grab John or Caroline and kiss them as they came out of the house. Others tried to carry ladders across the lawn so they could peer into the Kennedys' bedroom windows.

After a few months of this, Jackie decided to move to New York City. New York had been her first home as a little girl, and she had always loved the city. This was where she wanted to bring up Caroline and John.

Jackie had money of her own now, because Jack's will had left her a trust fund with an income of $200,000 a year. She could afford to buy a large apartment on the Upper East Side, on Fifth Avenue, a few blocks up the street from her sister Lee. The apartment's windows looked out on Central Park, where Jackie had spent so many happy times. She took John and Caroline to play in the park and showed them where little Jacqueline Bouvier had marched up to the policeman.

Jackie also bought a country estate in nearby New Jersey, where she stabled horses and took her children to ride on weekends. Bringing up her children seemed to be the only thing that mattered now. Jackie was especially grateful for Robert Kennedy's support.

Of all Jack's brothers and sisters, Jackie had always felt closest to Robert. Although he had several children of his own, he also looked after his niece Caroline and his nephew John like a father. And he was a good friend and advisor to Jackie.

During the next few years, Jackie traveled compulsively, as if she could somehow leave behind the fact that her husband had been brutally murdered. With movie stars and other celebrities of the "jet set," she flew to Europe, South America, Hawaii, Mexico, Canada, and Asia, as well as to the U.S. resorts of Aspen, Newport, and Hyannis Port. But all the parties and glamorous trips could not distract Jackie from the horror that haunted her. Nervous and short-tempered, she smoked more than ever and bit her fingernails. She longed to feel secure.

When Jackie was away, Caroline and John often stayed with their grandparents Janet and Hugh Auchincloss at Hammersmith Farm. Sometimes Jackie took the children with her for vacations in Hawaii or Ireland. If she traveled during the school year in New York, the nanny and other servants looked after Caroline and John.

In the spring of 1968, Robert Kennedy decided to run for president. Jackie was afraid for him, as were many other people. That April, the civil rights leader Dr. Martin Luther King Jr. was assassinated. Jackie had always supported and admired Dr. King, and she was stunned at his death.

That June Robert Kennedy won the California presidential primary election, and his prospects for winning the presidency seemed bright. But at the very celebration for this victory, he too was shot by an assassin. Now Jackie was shaken almost to the point of falling apart. "I hate this country!" Jackie told a friend. "I don't want my children to live here anymore. If they're killing Kennedys, my children are number one targets."

Even if Caroline and John weren't actually in danger, it was impossible for them to live a normal life. The public would not leave them alone. One day when Jackie was in Central Park with young John, a photographer jumped out of the bushes. John swerved and nearly crashed his bike.

In July 1969, as Jackie turned forty years old, the Apollo 11 mission made the first manned landing on the moon. The moon mission had been President Kennedy's idea, and Jackie's pride for him was mixed with sorrow. For her, the only legacy of the Kennedy presidency seemed to be danger and maddening, never-ending publicity.

Working Woman

More than ever, Jackie longed to be with someone who would cherish her and make her feel secure. In October 1968, she married the Greek shipping tycoon Aristotle Socrates Onassis. Ari, as his friends called him, was fabulously wealthy and fabulously generous. He loved to have a good time and to have his friends enjoy themselves. Jackie had known him as a comforting, reassuring friend for several years, but she only had started dating him seriously in 1968.

Cardinal Cushing of Boston, who had married Jackie and Jack Kennedy, refused to criticize Jackie's second marriage. Even Jack's mother, Rose, was understanding. But the public was not happy for Jackie. Most Americans, and most people around the world, wanted to keep on thinking of Jackie as President Kennedy's widow. How dare she go on with her life? How dare she marry Onassis, a short, not-very-good-looking foreigner, old enough to be her father, with a reputation for shady business dealings? If queenly Jacqueline had to marry again, they felt, she ought to have chosen a kingly man.

Jackie had chosen a man she thought would protect her and her children from danger. At the same time, she had no intention of giving up her independence. Ari agreed that she would live exactly the way she wanted to, and he would do the same. Jackie kept her Fifth Avenue apartment in New York, where Caroline and John went to school. On weekends Jackie and the children rode in the New Jersey countryside.

During school vacations Jackie and Caroline and John joined Ari on his 303-foot yacht or on his private Greek island, Skorpios. Ari reveled in entertaining his friends at lavish parties, but Jackie often preferred to go off by herself and read. She still loved the same kinds of books she'd enjoyed ever since she was a girl: fiction; books on art, ballet, or history; biographies; poetry.

Jackie expected that her new husband, with all his wealth, could protect her from publicity. After all, in Jackie's view, the point of being rich enough to own your own private island was that you could have real privacy. You could sunbathe nude on the beach, if you wanted to.

But Jackie was mistaken. On one of her visits to Skorpios, a team of photographers anchored their boat offshore and lay in wait for her. As she relaxed on the beach without her bathing suit, they swam from the boat in diving outfits. With underwater cameras and telephoto lenses, they caught several embarrassing pictures of Jackie. Even Ari Onassis, with his fabulous wealth, could not stop the tabloid papers from publishing them.

In 1973 Aristotle Onassis's only son and heir died in a plane crash. Ari was crushed by this blow, and his health suffered. In March 1975 he died in Greece. Jackie had never felt the need to explain her marriage to a prying public, but now, for Ari's sake, she told the press how much her second husband had meant to her: "Aristotle Onassis rescued me at a moment when my life was engulfed with shadows."

When Aristotle Onassis's estate was settled, Jacqueline Kennedy Onassis received $19 million. If she had wanted to, Jackie could have spent the rest of her life on shopping sprees, at parties, and on vacations. But Jackie wanted to do something meaningful with her life. Even before Ari's death, she had thrown herself into the fight to save Grand Central Terminal in New York. This famous building, a national landmark, was scheduled to be torn down and replaced with an office building.

The idea made Jackie very angry. Grand Central was one of the most beautiful and best-known buildings in the city. It rightfully belonged to the people—to the half million daily commuters and all the other travelers who passed through the station. It would be a shame if they were no longer able to walk under the vaulted ceiling of the rotunda, or meet friends at the four-sided clock, or climb the marble steps of the Grand Staircase, modeled on the staircase at the Paris Opera.

Jackie cared so much about Grand Central Terminal that she put aside her dislike of publicity and appeared at a press conference. She knew that the media might not pay much attention to the plight of Grand Central, but they'd cover any story involving Jacqueline Kennedy Onassis. So Jackie used her fame to get her message into newspapers and on radio and television. "A big corporation shouldn't be able to destroy a building that has meant so much to so many for so many generations," she said at the press conference.

Caroline and John, now in their teens, were impressed that their mother was working so hard for Grand Central Terminal. They saw the letters she wrote Mayor Abe Beam and other influential people in New York. Jackie had been writing such letters ever since she was a young girl, using a combination of flattery and suggestion to get what she wanted. "John and I always felt sorry for people on the receiving end of those letters," said Caroline later, "because what choice did they have but to do exactly what she asked?"

Saving historic buildings was good in itself, but Jackie realized she wanted full-time work, work that would make good use of her talents. By the fall of 1975 there was a new climate in the country. The states were in the process of deciding whether to ratify the Equal Rights Amendment to the U.S. Constitution, which would forbid discrimination against women. Women—including Jackie—were realizing that they could lead independent lives, doing whatever work they were capable of.

This was far different from the climate of the 1950s, when Jackie felt her choices were to get married or to end up as a housemother at Miss Porter's School. Now Jackie told a friend, "I have always lived through men. Now I realize I can't do that anymore."

During this time Jackie's former social secretary, Letitia Baldridge, was writing a book to be published by Viking Press. "What about publishing?" she suggested to Jackie at lunch one day. Jackie already knew the president of Viking, a college friend of her stepbrother Yusha's. Books were a lifelong passion for Jackie, and the idea of working with them appealed to her very much.

So in September 1975 Jackie went to work as a consulting editor at the Viking offices in midtown Manhattan. The first book she published was *Remember the Ladies: Women in America, 1750–1815*. It showed how American women of the eighteenth century had lived and worked, and their contributions to the growth of the country. The timing was perfect for this book to be published in 1976, the bicentennial of the founding of the United States. And Jackie was the perfect editor of this book, with her deep understanding of history. She also knew from her personal experience that women had always contributed to great events, even when they got no credit for it.

Jackie's life had entered a new stage. Caroline was studying in London for a year before going off to college, and John was about to leave for boarding school at Phillips Academy in Andover, Massachusetts. At home in her New York apartment, Jackie jogged around the Central Park Reservoir and practiced yoga. She could have appeared at some glamorous New York City social event every night, but she spent most evenings reading or with a few friends. One of her good friends was Maurice Tempelsman, who was also her financial advisor.

Keeping Jackie's private life private was as much of a problem as ever. On the street she wore big dark glasses and covered her hair with a scarf, but people recognized her anyway. Photographers stalked Jackie, waiting outside her apartment building or around her favorite shops and restaurants to snap a picture. Every new picture of Jackie O, as the tabloid papers called her, was worth big money.

At Viking Press, and later at another publisher, Doubleday, Jackie was happy to forget about her celebrity. "One of the things I like about publishing," she said, "is that you don't promote the editor—you promote the book and the author." Concentrating on her work, Jackie brought to bear all her passion for art and history, the "real hunger for knowledge" she had felt ever since childhood. She thought only about her job as editor, and she enjoyed every stage of it: deciding what book to publish, encouraging the author to write the manuscript, choosing the illustrations, designing the cover, planning the publicity.

Some of the books Jackie edited were beautifully illustrated volumes, like the ones she used to pore over as a little girl. *In the Russian Style,* for instance, showed the way Russians dressed—clothes, headdresses, jewelry—before the 1917 revolution. Many of her books were novels. Some books reflected Jackie's interests in ballet or French history.

Jackie's authors loved her. "She was the most extraordinary editor—involved in every aspect of the book's life," said Eugene C. Kennedy (no relation to the Boston Kennedys). Jackie suggested to him that he write a biography of Mayor Richard J. Daley of Chicago. Since she knew Mayor Daley from her days of campaigning with Jack Kennedy, she helped Eugene Kennedy get to know the mayor and persuade him to agree to the biography.

Jackie's style as an editor was like that of a sports coach, urging on her authors to do their best. "She had a gift for inspiring insecure authors," said one of them. All her authors felt lucky to have an editor who was so "fiercely bright and talented," as Eugene Kennedy commented. And Jackie felt lucky to be working on book after fascinating book, expanding her mind as she went. She said, "Each book takes you down another path."

An Example of How to Behave

Ever since the birth of her half sister, Janet, Jackie had enjoyed little children. When Caroline Kennedy married museum designer Edwin Schlossberg in 1986, Jackie looked forward to grandchildren. Jackie's first granddaughter, Rose, (named after Caroline's grandmother Rose Kennedy) was born in 1988. A second granddaughter, Tatiana, followed two years later, and a grandson, John, in 1993.

These grandchildren were the delight of Jackie's life. She took them for walks in Central Park, for rides on the merry-go-round, for ice cream cones. The joyful New York outings with her father and Lee seemed to live again.

As a girl at East Hampton, Jackie had written of her longing to live by the sea. Since then she had lived at the Auchincloss home by the sea, Hammersmith Farm, and at the Kennedys' home by the sea in Hyannis Port. In 1981 she decided to build a home of her own by the sea on Martha's Vineyard, an island off Cape Cod. It was on 375 acres, to give her privacy. The New England–style house was spacious, to put up all the friends and family she wanted to invite.

Jackie's son, John, graduated from Brown University in 1983 with a degree in history. He then went to New York University Law school and earned a law degree. Unlike his father, his uncles Robert and Edward, and his cousins Patrick, Kathleen, and Joe, John had no interest in becoming a politician. Sadly, his life would end at the age of thirty-eight in a plane crash. But Jackie would not have to suffer this tragedy, because it would not happen until after her own death.

Since she was a baby, Jackie had been strong and healthy. She took good care of herself, except that she had smoked cigarettes most of her life. In the summer of 1993 she began to feel tired all the time. She was still weary by the fall, but she kept on with her usual life. In Boston she appeared at the dedication of a new museum at the John F. Kennedy Library. She went riding in the country.

Later that fall Jackie discovered that she had non-Hodgkins lymphoma, an especially dangerous type of cancer. She fought the disease with chemotherapy and her typical courage, but she lived only a few more months. By May 1994 she was almost too weak to walk.

Still, Jackie managed to go to Central Park one more time. Her friend Maurice Tempelsman, Caroline, and Caroline's one-year-old, Jack, sat with her on a bench in the sunshine. "We'd better keep an eye on Jack," said Caroline. "He can't even talk yet—how could he go up to a policeman and say, 'My mother and my Grandma Jackie seem to be lost?'"

Jackie laughed. They were near that very place in the park where young Jacqueline Bouvier had marched up to the policeman. For a moment, that long-ago time seemed like yesterday.

A few days later, on Thursday, May 19, Caroline and John sat beside their mother's bed, holding her hands. Jackie died that night. As she wished, her funeral was held not far from her apartment, at the Church of St. Ignatius Loyola, where she had been baptized as a baby. She was buried at Arlington National Cemetery next to John F. Kennedy.

By the end of her sixty-five years of life, Jacqueline Bouvier Kennedy Onassis had accomplished great "feats of work and responsibility," as her grandfather Bouvier had put it. As First Lady, she used her passion for art and history to restore the White House. Thanks to her work, the president's mansion became a beautiful place for Americans to learn about their nation's history. *The White House: An Historic Guide* is still in print, after twenty editions.

Later, a private citizen but with the same love for history and beautiful things, she had fought to preserve Grand Central Terminal in New York and other historical buildings. "If you cut people off from what nourishes them spiritually and historically," she told the New York state assembly, "something within them dies."

As a book editor, Jackie had brought out the best in many creative people, guiding and encouraging them to do their finest work. One thing Jackie deliberately did not do, however, was write her own memoirs. "I want to live my life, not record it," she explained.

Perhaps Jackie's greatest achievement was the role she played in the days following the assassination of President Kennedy. No one could have blamed her if she had collapsed or stayed in her room. It was, after all, her husband who had been murdered as she sat beside him. She was the one who was left with two fatherless children.

In 1969, when Jackie was still in a state of shock over Robert Kennedy's death, one of her Bouvier cousins, John Davis, published a book about the family history. Several Bouviers were disbelieving and angry when Davis revealed that the Bouviers were not of "noble stock" at all. Michel Bouvier, the ancestor who came to America in 1815, was a cabinetmaker. In fact, he had actually made some furnishings for the White House: a table and chairs for President John Quincy Adams in 1825.

John Davis had also discovered that John Vernou, father of Michel Bouvier's wife Louise, had been a hairdresser and a tobacconist. There was no reason to think that these Vernous were related to the Vernou who had been knighted by Louis XIV of France, the Sun King.

In a way, though, it didn't really matter whether Jacqueline Bouvier was descended from French nobles or not. What mattered was that she had behaved nobly, at an agonizing moment of her life. During the weekend of President Kennedy's funeral, she had appeared on television, calm and courageous, before millions of Americans and others. She had shown them that her style went far deeper than designer clothes and lavish parties.

Through the ceremonies of those dark days, Jacqueline Kennedy had expressed her faith that life had a meaning beyond the tragedy of that moment. She had summoned all her self-discipline and strength of will—the same will that could control a powerful horse. She had held the country together by her example.

When Jackie was only a young student at Miss Porter's School, Grampy Jack had written her that she could become a leader. She must prepare herself, he had advised her, for that time. In November 1963 Jackie's time to lead had come. She had been ready. She had led her country in a way that would have made Grandfather Bouvier and all Jackie's ancestors proud.